In the COUNTRY of QUEENS

CARI BEST

Farrar Straus Giroux · New York

Farrar Straus Giroux Books for Young Readers
An imprint of Macmillan Publishing Group, LLC
175 Fifth Avenue, New York, NY 10010

Printed in the United States of America by LSC Communications,
Harrisonburg, Virginia
Designed by Elizabeth H. Clark
First edition, 2017

1   3   5   7   9   10   8   6   4   2

mackids.com

Library of Congress Cataloging-in-Publication Data

Names: Best, Cari, author.
Title: In the country of Queens / Cari Best.
Description: First edition. | New York : Farrar Straus Giroux, 2017 | Summary: In 1961,
    shy and overprotected eleven-year-old Shirley Alice Burns must begin speaking up if
    she is to do what she wants, including talking about her beloved, deceased father. |
    Description based on print version record and CIP data provided by publisher;
    resource not viewed.
Identifiers: LCCN 2016050911 (print) | LCCN 2017023594 (ebook) |
    ISBN 9780374370534 (ebook) | ISBN 9780374370527 (hardcover)
Subjects: | CYAC: Bashfulness—Fiction. | Family life—Fiction. | Death—Fiction. |
    Queens (New York, N.Y.)—History—20th century—Fiction.
Classification: LCC PZ7.B46575 (ebook) | LCC PZ7.B46575 In 2017 (print) |
    DDC [Fic]—dc23
LC record available at https://lccn.loc.gov/2016050911

Our books may be purchased in bulk for promotional, educational, or business use. Please
contact your local bookseller or the Macmillan Corporate and Premium Sales Department
at (800) 221-7945 ext. 5442 or by e-mail at MacmillanSpecialMarkets@macmillan.com.

For my father
And for A, P, and D
For MMF and MLR
And for my mother

TABLE OF CONTENTS

. . . . .

1 · A Lucky Day.............................3

2 · At Least Now I Know....................17

3 · In the Palace of Light.................28

4 · Dance, Ballerina, Dance................38

5 · The Difference Between Rich and Poor...48

6 · Pardon My French.......................55

7 · Minding Everybody's Business...........68

8 · Shirley's Winning Smile................81

9 · The Mickey Mouse Club Song Sung Sadly..86

10 · YCDBSOYA..............................92

11 · Digging Down Deep....................104

12 · The Egg That Broke the Chicken's Back... 113

13 · Opening Up...........................126

14 · In Absentia..........................134

15 · Taking Care of Business..............144

16 · The Last Supper......................151

17 · The Pony; the Twist; One, Two, Cha-Cha-Cha....158

18 · Children with Pug Noses..............173

19 · The Reason for Moving................177

20 · Smiling Back at the Great Spirit.....194

21 · Luke to the Rescue...................203

    Epilogue..............................208

Little friends may prove great friends.

—AESOP

Chapter 1
A LUCKY DAY

PERCHED ON THE EDGE OF THE STURDY SCHOOL CHAIR, HER SADDLE shoes anchored to the metal bar near the bottom, Shirley Alice Burns had high hopes that today would be a lucky day as she wrote in her best cursive at the top of the blue-lined, oatmeal-colored paper:

Shirley A. Burns   *June 16, 1961*
Class 6-1   *P.S. 606Q*
Spelling Test

Shirley smiled at the unusual number of sixes. She had always counted on six to be lucky ever since three sixes had won her the top prize in a contest when she was six. Her guess—666—had come closest to the actual number of buttons in the big jar at the Main Street Library. She pictured Miss Chin, the children's librarian, presenting her with a brand-new copy of *Eloise* by Kay Thompson, along with the jar of buttons. Shirley had opened the book and read the first sentence with delight—"I am Eloise I am six"—and her grandmother still used buttons from the jar when she needed to finish a blouse or a dress or some shorts she was sewing for herself, for Shirley, or for Shirley's mother, Anna. Shirley also loved the number six because her birthday was July 6th, and her father's was March 6th.

Last night, Shirley had studied the twenty possible spelling words for today's test at the dinette table in the company of Grandma, who sat quietly clipping the coupons she would present at the checkout the next time she shopped at Smilen Brothers Grocery, and Anna, who sat quietly polishing her fingernails. Shirley had referred to her mother as Anna since forever because Anna was not very Mom-ish. But never to Anna's face. The gluey smell of the fingernail polish, like Duco cement, was distracting, but Shirley tried hard to concentrate and not smell it.

After about twenty minutes, Shirley closed her notebook. "Thanks for not talking," she said to Grandma and Anna.

"What do you mean, *thanks*?" her mother asked, extending ten expertly polished coral fingernails. "Your job is to do well in school. My job is to work at Mr. Joseph's. That's the way it's been with us since Hector was a pup."

"And *my* job is everything else," Grandma piped up emphatically. "We are all on the same merry-go-round. We are all in the same world." Only Grandma said, "Vee are all on the same merry-go-round. Vee are all in the same vorld." Grandma was Russian and said her *w*'s like *v*'s.

Shirley sometimes thought her school job was the hardest, especially when there was a test. Tests gave her the jitters even when she was as well prepared as she was today.

Shirley put a lot of pressure on herself to achieve a perfect score on every spelling test. It was a hard-to-break habit, like her grandmother's habit of searching for treasures in garbage cans and her mother's habit of smoking Benson & Hedges cigarettes.

At 9:18 a.m. the test began.

"The first word is *stoic*," said her teacher, Mr. Merrill.

The more thoughtful members of Shirley's class, including Shirley, paused to think before they wrote. There was a no-erasing rule because Mr. Merrill said that people should trust their first instincts, which were usually correct.

Shirley was aware that she could erase daintily and not be noticed by the usual tattlers in the class—Lannie

Kaufman and Cynthia Sparks—but no erasing meant no erasing, and at school Shirley never did what she was not supposed to do.

After the class finished writing the first word, Mr. Merrill said, "The second word is *epitome*." This was followed by *abhorrence, audible, petrified, deceased, pivotal, gargantuan, penultimate*, and, finally, *pugnacious*— the ten moderately difficult words that Mr. Merrill had promised from the list of twenty.

Shirley thought the words were just plain difficult this week. Not moderately. Especially the bonus word, *acronym*, which wasn't even on the study list. She pictured the *nym* part of the word *synonym* and hoped for the best.

Ten seconds later, Mr. Merrill declared the test over. "Pencils down. Pass your papers forward."

Shirley fidgeted nervously at the finality of his words.

Then Mr. Merrill said, "There are only two weeks remaining in your sixth-grade careers, and almost every one of you has become a better speller since our first test back in September."

Shirley looked across the room at Maury Gordon. Maury was the absolute worst speller in the class, but still the nicest boy. Shirley saw his ears turn crimson. She was somewhat of an expert on the many shades a person could blush, since she did so herself with the same predictability as Grandma taking out her false teeth at night before bed.

Shirley wished Mr. Merrill had considered Maury's feelings before he spoke. But she could not undo what her teacher had done. What Shirley could do was be nice to Maury later on the bus ride home to Sparrowood Gardens, where they both lived.

Maury sat three rows over from Shirley, who shared her double desk with Barry-the-Brain Ben-David, the undisputed class genius. Their desk was in the last row, as far away from Mr. Merrill's as any of the thirty-six students' desks could be. At the start of the school year, Shirley hadn't been at all sure about her assigned seat in "Siberia," as Grandma would have called it. But she soon discovered some things she liked about sitting so far from the teacher. There was, of course, Barry-the-Brain, who was pretty nice overall and shared his Fritos with Shirley after lunch. It was too bad his hair had cornflake-size dandruff that dropped down onto his bushy eyebrows every time he moved.

Even better was watching what other kids in the seats in front of her were doing when they had no idea that anyone was looking. Like Marcy Bronson reaching into her desk for Milk Duds during silent reading and Lannie Kaufman removing a tiny rubber band from her braces and shooting it at Cynthia Sparks's Girl Scout uniform.

Or Beth Ann Lanier sneaking a note to Robin Miller this very second.

It was probably about the party tonight at Sharon Levitt's house, Shirley guessed. The one she wouldn't be going to, even though she had been invited, as she always was. Shirley's family didn't own a car—a wise thing for sure since her mother had never learned to drive and neither had her grandmother.

Anna wouldn't let me go even if we had a car and she knew how to drive, Shirley thought. *Or even if we lived within walking distance.* It was all about Anna's strictly enforced Safe-at-Home Doctrine, which Shirley respected but did not necessarily appreciate. Shirley wondered if Maury was going to the party.

Then, just as he did every week, Mr. Merrill called for volunteers to share their Listening Post essays on current events, which he had collected from the class on Tuesday and passed back now. He also sent their essays to the radio station WNYC so each could be considered for a Listening Post Award the following week. If you were a winner, your name was announced on the radio. So far, only one member of Class 6-1 had been recognized: Barry-the-Brain, back in April.

Shirley strategically positioned herself behind puffy-haired Jocelyn Needleman in case no one volunteered and Mr. Merrill randomly called on people. Fortunately, half the class raised their hands.

Shirley had chosen her topic from the *New York Post* that Anna had bought on her way home from work on Monday. Shirley went through the entire paper looking for a subject that interested her before returning to an article about a new organization that President John Fitzgerald Kennedy had established called the Peace Corps. Its purpose was to spread peace and understanding among the world's people. Serving in the Peace Corps was very appealing to Shirley.

It was the last Listening Post essay of the year, and Shirley had tried to make hers truly compelling. She had worked on it for hours.

"Peace and understanding are two vitally important elements that we need in order to survive. They are as vitally important as the air we breathe," she had written. "The Peace Corps will be a boon to mankind from its inception, and I intend to volunteer as soon as I am old enough. Writing these words today is my pledge to realize them tomorrow."

Shirley saved meaty words she read or heard spoken— like *boon, inception,* and *realize*—for future use. It was another habit of hers, one she saw no need to break.

She hoped that by the time she was eligible to

volunteer for the Peace Corps, she would be proficient in French, her favorite subject. Shirley included that in her essay, too. Then she named all of the exotic places (aside from France) where French was spoken: Mali, Morocco, the Congo, Switzerland, French Guiana, Algeria, Haiti, and parts of Canada. Then she wrote, "The word *corps*—pronounced 'core'—is even a French word. It means 'body.' The Peace Corps is a Body of Peace. The world can never have enough peace—or enough peace-loving people to spread it."

After some of her classmates shared their essays, Mr. Merrill said, "I want to stress how important it is that these essays are your own. That all essays you ever write are your own. Not your mother's. Not your father's. Not Walter Cronkite's. Not Ernest Hemingway's. Yours. I suspect that one student in the class is squirming in her chair this very minute for using someone else's words in her essay this week. That is called plagiarism—from the Latin *plagiarius*—meaning 'kidnapper.' In this case, a kidnapper of another person's words or ideas."

Everyone in Class 6-1 saw Mr. Merrill stare directly at Shirley. Some of them turned around and stared at her, too. Shirley saw Maury look down at his desk.

I know I am blushing the purple-red of a beet, she thought. She knew she should just stand up and say, Those *are* my words. Those *are* my ideas. Every one of them came out of *my* head and off *my* pencil. School is *my* job. Not my mother's. Not my grandmother's. Not Walter Cronkite's. Not Ernest Hemingway's.

But instead, Shirley said nothing and slunk so low in her seat that she could see into Barry's desk: pencils, erasers, a ruler, workbooks, textbooks, an extra pair of eyeglasses, *Microbe Hunters* for silent reading, the corner of a photograph.

The bell rang for lunch and Mr. Merrill collected the essays. Because it was Friday, the class ate at their desks so they could listen to WNYC broadcasting the past week's current events. At the end of the radio show, the Listening Post winners were revealed, but no one from Class 6-1 was mentioned. There had been a long drought since Barry-the-Brain.

Finally, it was time for recess.

Shirley's fingers rushed to the waist pocket of her dress, where a blue ball waited to be pulled out and slapped against the concrete handball wall in the schoolyard. Grandma sewed most of Shirley's dresses with a custom-made pocket for her ball—except when the dresses were hand-me-downs from Helen Katz, her aunt Claire's neighbor. Shirley stood up, eager to escape the stifling classroom and get outside.

But not so fast.

Mr. Merrill, holding a big manila envelope, was

11

lowering himself into the chair just vacated by Barry. "I would like a few words with you, Shirley," he said.

Shirley's best friend who was a girl, Edie Hill, wanted to stay behind with her, but Mr. Merrill said, "Please go outside, Edith. Shirley will join you shortly."

Shirley kept her hand in her pocket on top of the blue ball as she sat back down. She had never seen a person look as serious as Mr. Merrill did now—his face pink with purpose, his nostrils flared open like a dragon's.

"I am very disappointed in you, Shirley," said Mr. Merrill. "Your choice of words, the way in which you put them together, and the overall focus of your essay are not in character with anything you've ever written. Some of the writing is just too polished . . . too adult . . . to be your own. I want you to be the best writer you can be, Shirley, but plagiarizing is not the way."

Shirley wanted to explain how hard she'd tried to be different this time, but her throat tightened as if a boa constrictor had wound itself around it. Yes, she had read the newspaper article, but the meaty words she'd chosen were ones she'd been saving for a long time.

"Since you have no explanation, I will infer that you are aware that what you have done is equivalent to cheating and that you are sorry," said Mr. Merrill sternly.

Shirley stared at the big manila envelope, which said *Listening Post*.

"Still no answer?" asked Mr. Merrill. "You realize that I cannot send your essay to WNYC this week. It wouldn't be fair to the other students—or to you."

There was a long and agonizing pause.

Mr. Merrill then held out a piece of paper. "I am returning this to you."

Shirley saw that it was her essay, folded in half as if ashamed of itself. She reached out her hand to receive it.

"You are free to go outside now."

Shirley put her essay in a notebook and walked toward the door to the schoolyard. Untrue. Unfair. Unreasonable. She wished Mr. Merrill were Mrs. Greif, who came to school every Wednesday for the sole purpose of sharing her love of everything French with Shirley's sixth-grade class. Mrs. Greif thought Shirley's accent was *excellente* (French for "excellent"—say: "ec-say-lahnt"). Shirley thought everything about Mrs. Greif was *excellente*. She loved when Mrs. Greif called on someone in class, addressing him or her as *monsieur* or *mademoiselle*. It felt so grown-up. *Mrs. Greif would never accuse me of cheating,* Shirley thought, *when I did an assignment exceptionally well.*

Edie ran over to hug Shirley in the schoolyard. "Mr. Merrill can be so mean," Edie told her. "You're such a good writer, Shirl. You would never steal anyone else's words."

No, I wouldn't, Shirley thought. But she couldn't bring herself to say the words.

Shirley loved Edie. She didn't get to see her outside of school because she and Edie lived too far away from each other.

Edie and Shirley walked over to where Benny and Maury were playing handball. Of all the boys in the class, only those two didn't play easy just because Edie and Shirley were girls.

"What did Mr. Merrill want?" asked Maury, stopping the game.

"Nothing," said Shirley. "Let's just play."

So against the giant cement wall in the schoolyard, Shirley lost herself to handball for whatever time remained of recess. She expelled much of the anxiety she'd kept inside while she listened to Mr. Merrill accuse her of plagiarism. Of kidnapping. Because when Shirley played handball, nothing else mattered. Not a single thing.

I could beat the handball champion of the world, she thought, even though her fingers ached and swelled to the size of a baseball glove—which Shirley wished she had since she also loved to play baseball, but couldn't unless she borrowed someone's glove. Her mother insisted on buying her dolls and ballet slippers and bracelets and charms from fancy stores with the money she earned as a saleswoman at Mr. Joseph's Emporium of Fine Old

Things, but Shirley had never told Anna that she'd trade them all in two wags of a dog's tail for a baseball glove.

Shirley did not want to go back to the classroom when recess was over. But she had no choice. That was the rule.

On Friday afternoons, Mr. Merrill had two or three students read and talk about their book reports. Ronald Sackheim, who had one blue and one green eye, started with his. "*The Adventures of Tom Sawyer* by Mark Twain," he said confidently, knowing how much Mr. Merrill loved Mark Twain.

Shirley sat up in her seat; it was harder than a rock. But Mr. Merrill insisted that everyone practice good posture at all times, and Shirley was in no mood to be singled out again.

After Ronald, Shirley listened to Maury do his report on a book about Alexander Graham Bell.

When it was Barry-the-Brain's turn, he began, "*The Old Man and the Sea* was a very profound tale of strong wills."

Shirley heard one brilliant word after the next with admiration, but it was still hard to listen to when all she wanted to do was go home.

Shirley wished away the last minutes her watch said were needed to get to the end of that Friday afternoon, twisting the stem until it wouldn't twist anymore. *It's all wound up like I am,* she thought. She decided she might need to choose a new lucky number after all. *This could be the worst day of my life.*

But then Barry was concluding his report. *Hooray.* Shirley slid forward in her chair and planted her saddle shoes firmly on the gray linoleum floor. When the bell rang, she gathered her things and stood.

"See you all on Monday," said Mr. Merrill. "Happy Father's Day to all of your fathers." Mr. Merrill's dragon nostrils found Shirley as she filed out the door with the other kids who took the bus home.

Shirley smiled weakly at Mr. Merrill and thought, *Anna would want me to be respectful to my teacher, even when I don't want to be.*

Chapter 2
AT LEAST NOW I KNOW

SHIRLEY CLIMBED ONTO THE SCHOOL BUS AND SAT DOWN NEXT TO Maury. He always kept his tan book bag on the seat next to him and moved it to his lap only when he saw Shirley get on, even though their pesky neighbor, Beryl Abbie, a fifth grader who was the size of a third grader, tried to tug it onto the floor so she could sit next to him.

Maury talked nonstop about how much fun he and Shirley would have if they went roller-skating later.

"That's a really good idea," said Shirley.

"Let's change out of our school clothes and meet in the laundry room under your apartment. It'll be much cooler down there than it is inside this boiling bus," Maury said, wiping his sweaty forehead with the top of his hand. "I'm *so* thirsty."

"Me too," said Shirley.

Maury had no dandruff. He had a lot of auburn hair and a lot of auburn freckles and clean ears. He wore a plaid shirt with a tie that didn't clash, ate tuna fish for lunch, and was a whiz at science if not at spelling. Boys had to wear ties to school. Shirley was glad she wasn't a boy, although wearing a dress to school wasn't so comfortable either. Shirley wished she could go to Sharon Levitt's party with Maury tonight. She knew all about spin the bottle from Edie, but she herself had never played it. She was positive Maury would not wear a tie or smell like tuna fish at the party.

When the bus arrived at Sparrowood Gardens, Shirley, holding her books with her left hand and her red-and-black lunchbox with her right, waited her turn to jump down off the wide metal steps. Bus fumes, lawn mower exhaust, freshly cut grass, and the smell of Mrs. Kaplan's fish frying in Crisco welcomed her in the humid, buggy air as she landed on the sidewalk.

Shirley was so happy to see the Sparrowood Gardens sign and to smell the Sparrowood Gardens smells that she smiled for the first time in hours.

"See you later," she and Maury said at almost the same time. They lived at different ends of the small development, which was made up of about thirty brick apartments surrounding a grassy court. Each two-story building housed four separate families—two upstairs, two downstairs—with gardens in the front. Beryl Abbie, who lived three garden apartments away from Shirley, hung back to watch the tired bus as it dragged its old elephant self up the hill to the next stop.

Down the long driveway Shirley went, waving to Mrs. Farber walking her German shepherd, Candy, on the No Ball Playing field, where there were hundreds of mountains of fresh and decomposing dog droppings. Droppings that made Anna fly into a rage every time Shirley brought some home on her Keds, which she had done yesterday after playing baseball there using Maury's brother's glove.

Shirley also waved to Luke, the maintenance person in charge of all of Sparrowood Gardens' big and small problems. Luke was mowing the grass on the No Ball Playing field. He saluted her back. Shirley liked Luke. Everybody did.

A Paganetti's Sanitation truck dripped garbage juice on the street as it chewed up the contents of the big metal cans stored in the white-brick garbage house. Shirley wondered if Grandma had had any luck today picking through the cans for treasures. Shirley never cross-examined Grandma like her mother did. "Were you poking around in the garbage again, Mama?" Anna asked when she saw something new on the living room windowsill.

Shirley felt sorry for Grandma whenever Anna went on one of her rampages. It was part of the bond Shirley and Grandma shared, sort of like the common denominator Mr. Merrill taught about in math. She and Grandma were both in the same world. But most of the time, Shirley thought, Anna was in a different one.

"Not every vone is cut from the same cloth," Grandma liked to say. "Not even two fingers on your hand are the same."

Shirley examined her fingers carefully and agreed that no two were the same. Smart Grandma. She had an un-ordinary saying for everything ordinary.

It never ceased to amaze Shirley how brave Grandma and Grandpa had been to leave Russia and then Turkey on a crowded, smelly, rocking ship with their three little kids—Claire, Rosalie, and Anna—to come to America.

If it weren't for them, there would be no me, thought Shirley, *and none of my cousins either: no Arlene or Esther Marks and no Laurel, Ruthie, Steve, Phillie, or Scott Barrett.*

Shirley made her way through the shady breezeway under another section of apartments. Mrs. Evangelista, one of Sparrowood Gardens' Pigeon People—a group of elderly women who minded everyone's business, usually from a sunny bench—was seated on a brown lawn chair, her ample rear sagging like Santa's sack, across from a smoking Mrs. Steinman, another Pigeon Person, who looked like a skinny, barely active volcano. Their chairs left a narrow aisle for Shirley to pass through to the court and to her apartment.

Shirley went up the two steps of her stoop. She stopped to lift the top part of the mailbox that said BURNS/BOTKIN on the front—Anna and Shirley were the Burns part, Grandma, the Botkin—and took out the mail. Mustard, the old dog who lived next door, barked. Mr. Bickerstaff, Mustard's master, was away at work. Shirley had no idea what Mr. Bickerstaff did, except that when he walked Mustard he yanked too hard on the leash, which made Shirley gasp as if it were her own neck instead of Mustard's.

Grandma wasn't home, but the door to the apartment-green-colored apartment was unlocked. Shirley smelled her mother's stale Benson & Hedges cigarette smoke, Grandma's fresh but fake lily-of-the-valley perfume, and biscuits. Shirley guessed that Grandma was visiting her friend Augusta P, who lived next door to Beryl Abbie. Grandma and Augusta liked to play gin rummy and talk about the good old days when they were girls.

Shirley dropped her school stuff and the mail on the dinette table. There on the kitchen counter were freshly baked Pillsbury buttermilk biscuits with melted American cheese on top. She hungrily peeled the still-warm cheese, her favorite part, off one of the biscuits and ate it. Then she got herself an apple, a few Good & Plenty candies, and a spoonful of cherry vanilla ice cream from the freezer before going into the living room to check out Grandma's windowsill. Only one new thing sat there today—a perfect palm-size white china dog with orange-painted paws and ears, yellow eyes, black freckles and nose, and a big orange smile. It joined Grandma's other rescued things, including the one that Shirley was especially partial to: a woven metal picture frame with a big glass heart in the middle. The only thing missing was a picture.

"You wouldn't believe the things people put in the garbage," Grandma had once told her.

Shirley went into the bedroom she shared with her mother and moved her bicycle away from her closet door so she could get out her skates. She carried them by their leather straps to the dinette table.

Then she called her mother at work.

Anna's loud voice when she answered the phone— "Mr. Joseph's Emporium of Fine Old Things"—made Shirley feel as good as the warm, delicious cheese on top of the biscuits.

"I'm home," Shirley said.

"Iloveyou," said Anna, as though the three words were one.

"I love you, too," said Shirley, and hung up.

Shirley tried not to give in to the bad part of her day. When Mr. Merrill had accused her of plagiarism, that did not make it true, she thought. Next year she would be in junior high and, thankfully, there would be no Mr. Merrill.

Shirley noticed an envelope from Larry's Taxicab Company positioned on top of the pile of mail. Why did Anna get those envelopes? Shirley wondered every time one arrived. Whenever she asked about them Anna always said, "Those envelopes have nothing to do with you, Shirley." Shirley did know that her father, Donald Burns, used to drive a taxi. "Maybe he still does," she said out loud, "but since I haven't seen him in six years, I wouldn't know." There was that number six again.

Father. Shirley liked that word, though Anna's back went up like a cat's on her guard whenever Shirley said it. Anna's steadfast rule for the last six years had been to not call him anything. Certainly not Daddy or Dad or Pop or even Donald. And, heaven forbid, not Father. As if he had never existed. Of course, the very accepting Shirley Alice Burns accepted her mother's decree without even a feeble *why*. No one messed with her mom, Hurricane Anna, as unpredictable as a fiercely raging storm.

Someone should bring the Peace Corps to Sparrowood Gardens, Shirley thought.

Shirley tried to remember the three of them when they were the Burns family—Anna, Donald, and Shirley—before Grandpa died and Grandma moved in with them. She and her parents had lived in a small house in Valley Meadow and her grandparents had lived in the Bronx. But what came to her mind instead were the photographs she knew well—of her one-, two-, and three-year-old self standing alone in front of the house, on the sidewalk with a ball, in the garden holding a child-size shovel—black-and-white photographs that Anna had tucked into Shirley's album a long time ago. Shirley's favorite was the one that Grandma had taken after Shirley and Anna had moved to Sparrowood Gardens. Without her father. When he had started his Wednesday-afternoon visits. While Anna was away at work. The photo was of her four-year-old self sitting on a bench outside their garden apartment, her father's arm around her small shoulders. How lucky, Shirley thought, that she had that picture. For that reason, she kept it hidden behind the earlier ones, worried that Anna would tear it up if she knew where it was.

Shirley had never asked why her father hadn't moved to Sparrowood, too, although she constantly wondered. If only she knew where he was so she could tell him about

Mr. Merrill accusing her of stealing someone's words. Her father would understand completely; he would believe her; he would help her figure out what to do.

Shirley looked again at the envelope from Larry's Taxicab Company and felt empowered. Then she didn't. "I should. I shouldn't. I should. I shouldn't," she said as if she were pulling petals from a daisy. In the end, Shirley lifted the envelope off the pile. Very slowly and carefully, she began to unstick the flap without tearing it so she would be able to seal it back after she saw what was inside.

At last the triangular part of the envelope came unstuck.

Case #4017984 Donald Burns, deceased
    January 28, 1955
Plaintiff: Anna Burns, wife
Lawsuit filed against Defendant: Larry's
    Taxicab Company
Nathaniel Decker, Attorney

Shirley didn't understand most of what she had just read. So she read it again. She recalled that the word *deceased* had been on today's spelling test. How awful. Shirley believed in some coincidences. They happened for a reason, Grandma said. This must be the reason.

Then she realized in a panic that she needed to reseal the envelope right away. What if Grandma came home and found her reading her mother's mail? The next thing that came crashing down on her was that Anna had never let on that Shirley's father was dead. Did Grandma know? How about her favorite cousin and boy best friend, Phillie Barrett, who always told Shirley everything? Did he know, too? Who else knew? And why hadn't anyone told *her*?

Shirley sealed the envelope with a piece of Magic tape from the kitchen drawer since there was no adhesive left on the flap. She placed the envelope on top of the pile, then reconsidered and put it in the middle, hoping to draw less attention to it.

Shirley went to the window to look out at the space where her father used to park his Chevy on Wednesdays. At least now she knew he would never again visit her on Wednesdays or on any other day. At least now she knew not to wish he were here so she could tell him about her Listening Post essay. At least now she knew. Shirley took in a long, slow breath. Then she let it out. She did not cry. She *did* squeeze the blue ball in her pocket till her knuckles turned white.

Shirley had forgotten about Maury.

But no one was there when she ran down the ramp to the laundry room.

At least now she knew, Shirley thought again as she skated around and around on the smooth cement floor through the soapy water that leaked out from the bottom of one of the four washing machines. Sometimes Shirley liked to make wet circles or figure eights (she had tried sixes, but those were impossible) with the wheels of her skates. Other times, she pretended she was competing in the Roller Derby like the tough girls she watched on TV, elbowing their way around the track past the other girls. But not today. She didn't feel so tough today.

As Shirley coasted around the vertical pipe that held up the ceiling in the center of the room, she began to think that today might be a lucky day after all because now she knew the truth. Shirley crouched down low like a Roller Derby girl. She continued around and around like a tetherball, traveling the same distance from the pipe at every turn, her knees maintaining the momentum like it was second nature to her. Until Maury showed up.

"Hey, Shirl," he said. "How come you still have your school clothes on?"

Shirley looked down at her dress. "I was really busy," she answered, still thinking about her father and hoping that, one day, she wouldn't be afraid to ask why no one had told her he died.

Chapter 3
IN THE PALACE OF LIGHT

THE NEXT MORNING SHIRLEY FOUND HERSELF, AS SHE DID EVERY Saturday morning, in the apartment's hobbit-size bathroom, where Anna ordered her to serve a thirty-minute sentence "to clean yourself out before ballet so you can dance as light and as airy as a bird."

Shirley's ballet class began at noon.

Shirley didn't like it, of course, but she accepted the fact that on Saturday, much to her disappointment, her mother didn't work at Mr. Joseph's in Manhattan and was therefore home, where she could monitor Shirley's bathroom activities like a CIA agent.

Shirley heard Anna singing "You Made Me Love You" over the droning of the old Electrolux. Then she heard her drag a stepladder across the wooden floor to just outside the bathroom where an intricate cobweb lurked above the door. Shirley had blown on it on her way in to see how strong the spider was.

"I'll fix your wagon," Anna threatened the spider.

For heaven's sake, Shirley thought, *it's no bigger than a caraway seed.* But even tinier spiders scared Anna the way Mr. Bickerstaff scared Shirley when he yanked Mustard on the leash.

Shirley's elbow rattled the loose doorknob by accident.

Anna pounced. "Don't come out until you've done something, Shirley," she commanded. "You can do it," she added like a cheerleader with boundless enthusiasm for her team. Then finally, like a powerful mother superior, she warned, "I'll need to inspect before you leave."

Shirley knew about mother superiors from Monica Callahan, a girl Shirley's age who also lived in Sparrowood Gardens but who went to Our Lady Queen of Peace, a private school that Grandma said was supposed to make good girls out of bad ones. *Fat chance,* thought Shirley.

"Concentrate, Shirley," Anna advised as she dusted the photograph in the green leather frame on the dresser in the hall outside the bathroom door.

The photograph was supposed to be of Shirley's mother dancing with her father. Only her father had been skillfully scissored out, except for his right hand around her mother's waist.

Long ago when her Saturday-morning ritual began, the notion of wasting precious time in the bathroom had made Shirley's stomach act up. But one day, sitting back and concentrating on the tiled wall in front of her, Shirley realized that she could play a game using those twenty-five pink tiles.

Starting with the first tile, Shirley tried to find a sentence in which each syllable of each word landed on a different tile—with no tiles or syllables left over at the end. She sang every song she knew, tried every tongue twister and TV commercial. No luck. This exercise was definitely an exact science. Finally, after lots of singing (not too exuberantly or Anna would get suspicious), Shirley found her first winner—from *Pinocchio*, which happened to be her comfort movie even though it was definitely directed at kindergartners:

Star light, star bright,
First star I see to-night
I wish I may I wish I might
Have the wish I wish to-night.

And it was *parfait*! (French for "perfect"—say: "parfay"). Twenty-five syllables from start to finish with nothing left over at the end. From that time on, whenever Shirley took her Saturday seat in the bathroom, she delivered this poem to the Great Wall of Tiles before helping herself to a wish or two.

Shirley's first wish had always been to have her father back, but today she knew just how impossible that wish was. Her father was dead. Dead. Dead. Dead. He was not just in absentia like Anna claimed he was whenever she asked—unless *absentia* meant "dead land," which she knew it did not. *I am fatherless for real,* Shirley thought, *though no one ever said I was.* No one talked about it. No one said the word *dead* because it was not fun to say like *doughnut* or *dog* or *Dastardly Dan.*

Steeped in reality and sensible as she was most of the time, Shirley summoned up her second wish, which couldn't have been more different.

"Since I can't have my first wish," she whispered, "then I respectfully wish wish wish wish wish wish that I could go to Lake Winnipesaukee with the Barretts this summer." The Barretts, who lived about a mile away, were Aunt Rosalie and Uncle Rod and Shirley's cousins, including Phillie. Every year, Shirley got a pretty postcard from the Happy Hacienda at Lake Winnipesaukee in New Hampshire. Last summer's postcard said:

Dear Shirley girl,
This place is heaven. The sky and the water are the
same color: azure. There is no rain in sight today. But

who knows! Only mountains of trees in the distance
that look like broccoli.

Love,
Aunt Rosalie, Uncle Rod, Laurel, Ruthie, Steve & Scott

Of course, there was a separate postcard from Phillie:

Hi S,
I'm in a blue canoe on Lake Winni Pee. Wish you
were, too.

From P.B.

Shirley especially liked Phillie's postcard because
it explained that Winnipesaukee meant "Smile of the
Great Spirit." She guessed everything was azure at Lake
Winnipesaukee: the sky, the water, and even the canoes.
She would wear her new azure bathing suit, which she
would ask Anna for the next time they went shopping.
She couldn't pull the old skimpy one up any more to cover
the top of her without exposing her cheeks on the bottom.

No one knew how much Shirley wanted to see heaven
and the Smile of the Great Spirit and sit in a blue canoe on
Lake Winni Pee except for Phillie. Phillie also knew how
much Shirley hated being a too-old camper at Breezy Bay

Day Camp, where she would get a Clean Plate Award for eating all of her spaghetti with meat sauce that looked like blood and guts. And make unnatural nature projects from pine cones and acorn tops with sticky, runny Elmer's glue that turned all white and hard and bumpy when it dried.

Shirley knew that going to Lake Winni Pee was one thing she could fix if she just spoke up. "Which I plan to do one day soon," she whispered to herself. "When my courage comes in. Or I'll be like Pippi Longstocking, whose courage never leaves her plucky self. Ever." *Pippi Longstocking* had been Shirley's comfort book ever since she'd first read it in second grade. Comfort came from different directions in especially trying times.

"Aunt Rosalie," Shirley practiced, "I've wanted to go with you guys to Lake Winnipesaukee for a long time. But I never told you because I realize I'm not part of your immediate family and this is your annual summer vacation, and if you wanted me to come, you would have invited me yourself. But I know I'd love it and you wouldn't have to worry about me drowning because I got a swimming award when I was eight at Breezy Bay Day Camp, which I wouldn't have to go to this year if I went to Lake Winnipesaukee with all of you."

But until she worked up her courage, Shirley would have to settle for a wish—that the Barretts would invite her to go with them. That really wasn't so bad because a person never knew when a wish would magically turn into the real thing. Like when Phillie wished for his very own pet to go along with the Barretts' dog, Porky, who belonged to everyone in his family. Harry, the amazing and exotic Brazilian piranha, appeared a few days later in a bowl on Phillie's doorstep. Complete with fish food and instructions from Mr. Hodges, the oil deliveryman, who had to move in with his daughter and her fierce fish-eating cat. Too bad for Mr. Hodges, but lucky for Phillie— and Harry, who got to go to Lake Winnipesaukee last year with Phillie and his family. *If my wish came true,* Shirley thought, *then I wouldn't have to speak up. Wouldn't that be something!*

Then feeling especially clever and suddenly as plucky as Pippi, Shirley made up her own tile game sentence: "My name is Shir-ley Al-ice Burns, and I am in here because my moth-er thinks she knows ev-er-y-thing." Twenty-five tiles, twenty-five syllables.

"Shirley, are you done?" Anna called. "Fifteen minutes until we have to get ready for ballet. Are you getting excited?"

"Almost," Shirley called back. Was she excited about going to ballet? No way. "But I am excited about lighting up the Palace!" she whispered, reaching for some matches that Anna kept on a shelf for when she needed to smoke a Benson & Hedges.

At first Shirley had trembled at the idea of striking a match because she was afraid she might burn her fingers, her knees, or the beauty spot on her left thigh. But after lots of practice, she was now an expert. First she opened the window so Anna wouldn't smell anything. Then she placed six sections of White Cloud toilet paper in the sink. She took out a match and closed the matchbook cover before striking the red tip and lighting an impressive fire in the sink. Shirley quickly blew out the match and announced quietly, *"Voilà!"* (French for "There it is!"—say: "vwa-la"). "The fabulous Shirley Burns has worked her magic once again, transforming a dreary bathroom into a veritable Palace of Light!"

If anyone ever discovered that I, the shy and mousy Shirley Alice Burns, lit a fire in the bathroom, Shirley thought, *I would be in big trouble.*

Shirley looked down at her watch. Thirty minutes would soon be history. She found the small Phillips screwdriver that she kept hidden behind the toilet. She tightened the loose doorknob from inside the bathroom the way Luke once showed her. Then she noticed that the shower curtain was lopsided because one of the plastic rings had come apart. Standing on the edge of the bathtub, Shirley tugged up the curtain and snapped together the ends of the ring through the perfect hole-punched opening at the top. She checked the bathtub for spiders—to save Anna the trouble and to spare her own ears: Shirleeey, I need you to get this monster out of here this second before it kills me! But there were no spiders; there was only one measly moth that unfortunately turned to dust in Shirley's fingers as she attempted to let it go free out the window.

"Sorry, buddy," said Shirley.

Shirley wished she could fix everything. But some things were just not fixable. "I understand that," she whispered. "Like I can't fix my father so he isn't dead. Or the photo of my mother dancing without him because I don't have the missing piece. Or Anna so she isn't so stormy. Or myself because I am a perennial chicken like Grandma's perennial sweet william that comes back every year in her flower garden."

Shirley could hear Anna crooning like Frank Sinatra this time: "Do dooo doooo, do doo do do do do doooo . . ."

She stuck her feet into her bunny slippers, which were the same soft, fuzzy material as the bath mat and the toilet seat cover, and tied her robe around her pink kitten pajamas, sewn by Grandma. Then she closed the window, wiped up what was left of the ashy fire with some downy White Cloud, dumped the toilet-paper-and-ash lump into the toilet, flushed, opened the door, and told Anna that it completely slipped her mind to call her in to inspect.

"Are you sure you did something, Shirley?" Anna asked, sounding concerned.

"Yes, Mom. I did lots of things," said Shirley, sounding confident.

It's too bad that I'm only brave in the Palace of Light, she thought. *But now I have to get ready to catch the first of two buses to Madame Makarova's Royal Academy of Ballet for unaspiring ballerinas like* moi. (French for "me"—say: "mwah.")

"You're so lucky, Shirley," said Anna as Shirley pulled on her black leotard. "I wish *my* mother had given *me* ballet lessons." She handed Shirley her round patent-leather case with the perfect pink ballerina stenciled on the front.

Grandma, hugging Shirley goodbye, had clearly heard Anna's lament but didn't say a word. Nobody messed with Hurricane Anna. Not even Hurricane Grandma.

Chapter 4
DANCE, BALLERINA, DANCE

IF SHIRLEY HAD HER WAY, THE ROUND BLACK PATENT-LEATHER case with the butter-soft Capezio ballet slippers inside would roll into the aisle of the bus toward the fancy lady with the Barricini chocolate shopping bag who was patiently waiting by the door to get off.

The fancy lady would try to stop the ballet case from rolling with her foot, but would just miss. Anna would cry for help as if a thief had run off with the secondhand designer purse that she had gotten on layaway at Mr. Joseph's. Shirley would ask, "How could that have happened?" and pump her heel up and down to give Anna the impression that she was trying her hardest to free her shoe from a mound of gum on the floor. But actually, Shirley would chase after the case when and only when she looked out the window and saw it lying in the street, flattened like one of Grandma's potato pancakes.

"It was a freak accident," Shirley would tell Anna, once she was back on the bus.

When they arrived at the bus stop where the next bus would be waiting to take them to Madame Makarova's Royal Academy of Ballet, Anna would tell the driver sadly, "We are not going to ballet class today, Vince." Then Shirley and Anna would have to go all the way home again. *Can't do ballet without my Capezio slippers. How perfect would that be?* Shirley asked herself smugly.

Truthfully, Shirley dreaded her Saturday ballet classes so much that to make herself feel less anxious, she had secretly taken to calling her teacher Madame Macaroni. A name much more fitting, since Shirley had absolutely no aspirations to prima ballerina–dom. But try to explain that to Anna, Shirley would not, not in a million years. In fact, that very ballet case with the pink ballerina stenciled on the front was securely positioned between Shirley's feet. She looked out the window. "Blech," she mumbled. "We're almost there."

"You know," said Anna, pointing with her chin to the ballerina on the case, "I could have been like her. Look at these long arms, skinny legs, and strong toes." Anna gracefully extended her extremities.

Shirley looked over even though she'd seen Anna's extremities and witnessed their boundless grace many times a day for almost twelve years.

"If I couldn't be a ballerina," Anna said, sighing wistfully, "then I wanted my little girl to be one."

Whether I like it or not, Shirley thought, remembering how, since she was five, Anna had coached her to stand as straight as an arrow, stretch her knees like a rubber band, be as floaty as a feather on her feet, and make her hands wavy like wings instead of stiff like wires.

. . . . .

When the class began, Madame Makarova pounded out chords on an old upright piano as she bellowed, "First position, second position, all with grace."

First base, second base is where I want to be, Shirley told herself, longing for the No Ball Playing field at Sparrowood Gardens. Shirley stifled a laugh, but she had to be careful. If Madame Macaroni didn't catch her chortling, Anna would, watching every choppy pirouette through the one-way mirror. Some handy person like Luke had installed it so that parents paying a lot of money could watch a class of mostly ungraceful children trying to appear graceful.

Shirley would have traded places with Anna in two

wags of a dog's tail. She pulled her leotard out in the back. The elastic made a loud snapping sound that caught the attention of Madame Macaroni, who was adjusting someone's arabesque. Shirley looked sheepishly away.

As she went up-down, up-down, holding on to the rigid ballet barre, she promised herself she would not fail her mother. After all, if Anna could walk over the bridge to the subway on workday mornings instead of taking the bus, if she could bring her lunch and not buy it at the automat downtown, and if she could resist the alluring Marcella Borghese lipsticks in the window of Woolworth's just to pay for ballet lessons, then Shirley felt she had no right to be a spoiled brat and complain.

Shirley's dance classes were the only things Anna managed to save her money for. Anna was forever laying away one thing or another from Mr. Joseph's to make their crummy apartment into a mini museum. This month's purchases included a big jade ashtray with wooden legs and a ceramic statue of a smiling Bambi whose head Anna's friend Hal decided was the perfect place to hang his hat whenever he and his cigar came for a visit— which was way too often, in Shirley's opinion.

The thought of Hal made Shirley's blood boil. She did deeper knee bends, held her legs extra-straight, jumped higher than she'd ever jumped before, and sweated.

"Good hard work today, Shirley, my ballerina girl!"

praised Anna when they met in the waiting room after class. Shirley beamed.

As she and Anna walked to the Stationhouse Diner for lunch, Shirley daydreamed about the attached house she was saving for her and Anna and Grandma to live in. There would be plenty of room for Anna's layaways, Grandma's sewing stuff, and her own dioramas, which at the moment were lined up under her bed due to a serious lack of private space in the bedroom that she shared with Hurricane Anna.

In the meantime, Anna was forever short of money and Shirley usually had to lend her some till payday. Shirley had the money to lend because she saved the two-dollar allowance she got each week from Hal. The trouble was that if Shirley didn't thank Hal profusely, Anna would poke her under the Sunday dinner table to remind her. Shirley tried not to let that happen, even though she didn't want to talk to Hal about anything—much less thank him.

"Don't you adore ballet?" Hurricane Anna asked at the Stationhouse Diner, having just blown away a lady who tried to sit next to her at the counter because Shirley hadn't been nervy enough to put her rear on the seat first.

"I like ballet," Shirley answered, blushing raspberry red at the sound of her untruth. She couldn't quite bring herself to utter the word *adore* but had to admit she was pleased at Anna's smile.

"Don't forget that Hal's coming over for Father's Day dinner tomorrow," Anna said.

Hal's job was to fill store windows from Brooklyn to Bridgeport with props to lure people in to buy new shoes, samples of which he generously brought on his Sunday visits. The back of Hal's van was strewn with creepy mannequin parts: a leg here, an arm there, a head that rolled whenever Hal took a turn on three wheels, which he did all the time. Pails, shovels, sand, and beach umbrellas also abounded. The summer season was upon Hal.

Every time Shirley thought about Hal, she wished he would keep driving. Maybe to Boston or to Burlington. Or even to Bismarck. Without ever stopping in Queens.

"How can I forget?" mumbled Shirley.

Lunch—grilled cheese sandwiches with dill pickles and potato chips—arrived in an open-top hopper car, third in the long line of Lionel trains that circled the perimeter of the Stationhouse Diner's counter. It was Shirley's very favorite place to go after ballet. The trains were like the ones Shirley's dad had brought her, only much bigger.

After lunch, Anna and Shirley took the two buses home to Sparrowood Gardens. Grandma was outside reading her Russian newspaper. Shirley bent to kiss her. Anna wiggled her fingers in a dramatic wave hello.

When they got inside the apartment, Anna went into the kitchen to call Aunt Claire to confirm what time everyone—the Barretts included—should gather for their usual Saturday dinner.

Shirley went into the bedroom. She dragged the stepladder over to Anna's tall dresser, climbed up, and with great care lifted a big brown box from the top of it. With greater difficulty, she carried it down the rickety steps, putting two feet together on each step like Markie, her baby neighbor, did when he first learned to walk.

Inside the box were the cars of her Lionel train set, the cardboard tunnel, the sections of track, the transformer, and the tiny metal figures that waited on the platform for the train. Shirley smiled. She was always happy to see them; it was as if they were her long-lost family: mother, father, brother, sister, grandma, grandpa, dog.

Even though Shirley had had a very easy time setting up the trains with her father on Wednesdays, it was touch and go for her on her own to connect the track sections so that electricity would flow through, to get the cars to stay coupled together, and to place the tunnel exactly right so it wouldn't topple over. Shirley had been fearful of electricity ever since she was four, when she'd put the other end of the cord to Anna's plugged-in Gillette shaver in her mouth to see what would happen—and felt her entire body buzz all over. So now, after she'd set up the train, Shirley plugged the transformer into the outlet with her eyes closed. But the train did not start.

The last time she'd wanted to play train, Shirley had had to call Phillie to come over and help her get everything going. But she didn't want to call him today because she was still mad that he hadn't told her that her father was dead. She wasn't 100 percent sure he knew, but she was 99.9 percent sure. Why else had Phillie once said that his mother, Aunt Rosalie, thought Shirley was a poor girl? Now it made sense.

When her mother had finished talking to Aunt Claire, Shirley decided she would call Maury instead. He might smell like tuna fish, but Shirley didn't care. Maury was good at putting train tracks together, and he was cute. Most important, she didn't think he knew her father was dead—at least, he never acted like he knew; he never felt sorry for her.

"I just have to finish my tuna sandwich," Maury said when Shirley called, "and I'll be right over."

Once he got there, they took turns being the conductor and the whistle-blower.

"We can go to Lake Winnipesaukee for a swim and a huge sundae," said Shirley, drawing out the *u* in *huge*. "One of those make-it-yourself sundaes you can get at

Kellerhaus. Everything costs the same there no matter what it weighs," she added with authority, since she'd heard it all from Phillie. "I'm making a giant dish with pistachio ice cream, strawberries, chocolate chips, bananas, pineapple, coconut flakes, and butterscotch syrup."

Maury said, "I'm having chocolate with chocolate sprinkles, Bosco syrup, and lots of marshmallows."

Then they got so hungry for real ice cream that they made a mad dash to the refrigerator.

"I am pleased to say that we have two delicious flavors to choose from today: cherry vanilla and butter pecan," Shirley said, looking into the freezer.

She got out two bowls, an ice cream scoop, and two spoons, then dropped two generous balls of ice cream into each bowl.

"Mmmm," Maury said, his mouth full of butter pecan.

"Yummm," Shirley said, her mouth full, too, but with cherry vanilla.

Feeling especially happy, Shirley asked Maury about Sharon Levitt's party.

"I didn't go," said Maury, "because you didn't go."

Shirley was delighted.

Then Beryl Abbie knocked on the screen door and Shirley invited her in to play train, too. At first Beryl

Abbie wanted to toot the whistle, but then she wanted to be the conductor.

"Slowly but Shirley, the train approached the station," Beryl Abbie announced in a low, ghoulish voice, cupping her mouth over the loud *choo-choo*s. She didn't have a Queens accent, so the way she said *surely* made it sound like *Shirley*.

Shirley wanted to correct her, "You mean 'slowly but surely,' don't you, Beryl Abbie?" But sometimes the littlest things got Beryl Abbie riled up, so Shirley didn't say anything.

Maury did, though. Curling his hand around his ear, he said, "Your mom is calling you, Beryl Abbie."

Even though she wasn't.

Chapter 5
THE DIFFERENCE BETWEEN RICH AND POOR

AFTER MAURY LEFT, SHIRLEY GATHERED UP HER LIBRARY BOOKS, looped a Macy's shopping bag over the right handlebar of her bike, and dropped the books in. She wheeled the bike through the bedroom, down the short hall, past the dinette table, and across the living room rug, where Anna was ironing her dinner dress and Grandma was looking for her sandals.

"See you in a while," said Shirley. She held on to the handlebar with one hand while she opened the door to the outside with the other and bumped the bike down the two front steps. "Bye, Mustard!" Shirley called when the dog barked his greeting from inside his apartment.

Shirley pedaled past the Pigeon People on the benches. Mrs. Evangelista and Mrs. Steinman sat among them.

They smiled and waved benevolently, even though Shirley was positive they started blabbing about her as soon as they saw she was far enough away not to hear. *But I have the equivalent of X-ray vision in my ears,* thought Shirley, *and I can hear every single word they say, including that remark I once heard: "Poor girl. Growing up without a father."*

Shirley now realized that Grandma must have spilled the beans to them. *But why didn't she spill them to me?* Shirley asked herself. *All I can say is, they're wrong. Aunt Rosalie is wrong, too. I am not a poor girl. I am, in fact, pretty rich.*

And here's why, Shirley thought as she pedaled. There was still a whole hour before the Main Street Library closed and before Miss Chin, the librarian, went home. Shirley loved Miss Chin.

Here is why else I am rich, Shirley mused as she rode. She was done with her Saturday bathroom and ballet duties for another week, she had a train set to share with Maury, she had a bike and a blue handball, and she had many more Saturdays to go to the library to borrow books. Especially the new ones that smelled so good, with their brand-new dust jackets, new paper, and new print.

Shirley had read how Pippi Longstocking, the strongest girl in the world, handled *her* fatherless situation.

Pippi was strong enough to pick up a horse and a cow and the muscle man at the circus without her father helping her, because he was in absentia, too—blown off the deck of a ship straight into the sea. And her father wasn't around to warn her about dancing with scary people like robbers, so she danced with them because Pippi felt in her heart that they weren't truly bad people. She made her own decisions.

From now on, Shirley would try to be strong like Pippi. After all, hadn't she carried that heavy-as-a-horse box with her trains all the way down from the top of the dresser by herself? Pippi said she would always come out on top. *But the difference between Pippi and me,* thought Shirley, *is that she makes sure she comes out on top. And I don't. Yet.*

Then Shirley thought about her mother. Anna could do whatever she wanted. However, she did not have a library card. She bought books and threw away the dust jackets because she thought dust jackets were dust collectors. But even if dust jackets were dusty, they were necessary so you could see what the book was about. A dust jacket had told her how Astrid Lindgren, who wrote *Pippi Longstocking,* had once been a girl like herself, except that she rode a horse instead of a bike because she lived in the country of Sweden, where there were dirt roads.

I live in the country of Queens, thought Shirley, *where there are asphalt roads.* She had read all that good stuff on the dust jacket that no one could remove because it was on a library book and the library law said you must never remove the dust jacket. Or else.

Actually, I am the richest person on earth by far, Shirley thought, *because Grandma is my grandma.* Grandma was the one who first took Shirley to the library to get a library card because, according to her, libraries were good inventions, like sewing machines and toilets.

The Main Street Library did not have Russian books, so Grandma had to buy them from the Russian bookstore near Macy's. Grandma's books were paperbacks with no tempting dust jackets for Anna to confiscate and throw away when she cleaned. But Shirley suspected that Grandma also had hardcover books that she hid under the mattress of the open-up couch she slept on. Grandma, who had once told Shirley, "I only vare eyeglasses to look smart," was smarter than anyone Shirley knew, with or without glasses.

Shirley walked into the library and sat down at one of the round tables in the children's section, inspired to write a letter. She took a piece of scrap paper and a tiny nub of a pencil from an old S&W green beans can sitting in the middle of the table and began:

June 17, 1961

Dear Astrid Lindgren,

I wish Pippi Longstocking was my sister. She
would tell me her secret to being brave, and I
would show her how to be sensible and not walk
backward when she could easily fall off a curb
into traffic. (It's good that there are no curbs
where Pippi lives.) Thank you for Pippi. Is
she made up or is she a real girl like you and
me? Will her lost father be found? (Mine
won't.) Pippi is as sweet as the treats she gives
her friends for no reason except that she likes
them. Even bank robbers. Pippi Longstocking
is a book for all ages. My grandma would like
it if she could get it in Russian.

Yours till the kitchen sinks, meaning forever,
because our kitchen has a very strong foundation
and will never sink.

Shirley Alice Burns

Shirley signed her name in her teeny-tiniest handwriting. *I am just a small nobody next to the great Astrid
Lindgren, who knows so much more about everything, including writing, than I do.*

Shirley put the letter in her shirt pocket, only to take it out a second later. She had no idea where to send it. So she approached Miss Chin's desk.

"Could you please send this letter to Astrid Lindgren in Sweden?" Shirley asked in a whisper.

"I'll try my best," answered Miss Chin.

"Thanks," Shirley said, still whispering.

Shirley selected her books, then walked over to the circulation desk, where she checked out *Pippi Longstocking* again and *The Borrowers* as well as *Cheaper by the Dozen*, which she'd seen on display in the junior high section. It was about a big family of kids and pets and a mother and father who did fun things together. This book was more appropriate for almost-twelve-year-olds, Shirley decided. But she would always love *Pippi Longstocking* best. Even when she was a hundred.

After Shirley left the library, she pedaled down a street with neat attached houses that had gardens with rose bushes and small brick patios with metal rocking chairs. *One day Anna, Grandma, and I will be rocking back and forth in metal chairs on our own brick patio in front of our own attached house,* she thought.

When she got back to Sparrowood Gardens, Shirley saw Grandma rummaging around inside the garbage house. She hoped that Anna hadn't seen Grandma in there, for Grandma's sake.

By the time Shirley pulled her bike up the steps, through the screen door, and into the bedroom, then put her library books on her night table, Grandma was back. Shirley heard Anna singing in the shower.

"There is only a little time before vee have to leave for Aunt Claire's, my sunny child," Grandma told Shirley as she rinsed an aqua-colored doll-size chair in the kitchen sink.

Shirley knew that one of Grandma's tiny found dolls would soon be sitting in that tiny chair, because empty chairs were just too sad to look at.

Chapter 6
PARDON MY FRENCH

SHIRLEY, ANNA, AND GRANDMA, ALL SHOWERED AND COIFFED AND dressed in their Saturday-evening finest, started off on their walk to Aunt Claire's attached house, about five blocks away. Grandma wore her newly sewn original creation—a dress with a pattern of turquoise and white polka dots. A kerchief to match was pulled over her bun and tied in back, above the familiar small orange-red earrings fastened to her big earlobes. Grandma was especially buoyant tonight.

"Yesterday Rudolf Nureyev, the greatest Russian ballet dancer ever, decided to remain in Paris and not go back to Russia," Grandma said, glowing with pride. "Just like me. I never want to go back to Russia either."

"I know," said Anna. "He defected. It was all over the news. Rudy is very handsome."

Shirley thought it rather amusing that Anna was on a first-name basis with a famous ballet dancer.

Grandma didn't speak much about what she called her escape from Russia. She once told Shirley that her mother and father and most of her eleven brothers and sisters had been wiped out in the Russian Revolution of 1917, and that she and Grandpa Sam had lived in Turkey for a few years before coming to America. Shirley also knew that Grandma never ate sardines to this day. "Vee vere forced to eat them every day on the crowded, freezing, dirty ship from Turkey, and I don't vant to remember anything about the vorst time in my life."

Grandma, now taking measured strides, said it felt like she was walking barefoot—her snazzy new sandals from Macy's were that comfortable.

Anna wore her tightest, narrowest, blackest dress, also sewn by Grandma. She had her hair in an upsweep, as she called it, with a hundred bobby pins, and had generously dabbed herself behind each ear with the special-occasion perfume that Mr. Joseph had given her for her last birthday. Shirley had watched the dabbing.

Anna is a fashion plate, Shirley thought, admiring her mother, who was a few steps ahead. *I am not.* Shirley was wearing her yellow-and-white skort—short enough to be shorts, but flouncy enough to be a skirt—and her poofy white blouse, both of which had also been bought at

Macy's. When Shirley walked, she sashayed a little; she liked what she was wearing, but she knew it was nowhere as *chic* (French for "stylish"—say: "sheek") as her mother's outfit.

Shirley's stomach fluttered with butterflies at the thought of seeing Phillie at Aunt Claire's, but she dismissed that thought in favor of the thought of seeing Aunt Claire's big black dog. Shirley had covered a small piece of hamburger from last night's dinner in Saran Wrap and tucked it in the pocket of her skort.

Aunt Claire was Anna's oldest sister, Grandma's oldest daughter. Both Aunt Claire's dog and her best friend were French. One was a poodle; the other was a *femme* (French for "woman"—say: "fahm"). The dog's name was Natalie; the woman's name was Huguette (say: "eww-get"). Natalie and Huguette could have been sisters. They had perfect haircuts, perfect skin, perfect perfume, perfect manners, and perfect pedicures. The fact that Hal was not invited to Aunt Claire's on Saturday nights made everything even more perfect. Or almost perfect—except for Phillie.

Tonight when they greeted each other, Anna and Huguette (also in her tightest, narrowest, blackest dress) kissed the air instead of each other's faces, maybe so they wouldn't smear their lipstick, maybe because they didn't really like each other. Shirley wasn't sure. She noticed that Grandma was having none of that kissy-kissy Huguette stuff. Grandma shook Huguette's perfect *main* (French for "hand"—say: "maaa," like the bleat of a goat, for about half a second).

When it was her turn to greet Huguette, Shirley said, *"Bonsoir"* (French for "Good evening"—say: "bone swahr"), hoping it would be enough. But Shirley got the air kissed around her, too, which was mortifying, especially since Phillie, who had a habit of popping up when she least expected him to, was watching and laughing behind Aunt Claire's sofa. Shirley shot Phillie a dirty sneer.

Phillie reacted with a soundless "What did I do?"

Aunt Claire unknowingly cut short the awkward moment between her niece and nephew by asking Shirley to take Natalie outside for a walk. Aunt Claire's dark, deep-set eyes reminded Shirley of two ominous caves that she was afraid to get too close to.

"Please make sure Natalie does her big business," no-nonsense Aunt Claire told her, "so that I won't have to be bothered with that later." To Phillie, Aunt Claire said, "Please make sure everyone at the table has a glass."

The other kids, Phillie's sisters and brothers—Laurel, Ruthie, Steve, and Scott—got their "Please make sure" assignments from scary-eyed Aunt Claire, too, and as usual, Aunt Claire's two princess daughters, Esther and Arlene, didn't get any assignments. Uncle Bill, who was their dad and also a lawyer, told people what to do all day at work, but when he was home, he happily sat back while Aunt Claire ran the show.

Shirley attached the rhinestone leash to Natalie's rhinestone collar, and the two galloped gleefully down the street to the park. Shirley gave Natalie the chunk of hamburger when they got there. Then she gave her lots of time to sniff tree trunks, fire hydrants, and chain-link fences. Natalie snapped at flies and tried to roll in a pile of something vile. Shirley gently but firmly pulled her away.

"You don't really want to do that, do you, Natalie?" Shirley asked. Natalie looked up.

I do, the dog implied.

But Natalie respected Shirley's reservations, and they moved on. When Natalie peed, she burned the healthy green grass on the side of the road almost instantly because it was still so hot out. But Natalie had no big business to do tonight. Maybe Natalie was afraid that if she stopped to squat, she'd miss out on a precious minute of fun with Shirley. So they ran some more, this time in a new place down a new hill, where Natalie sniffed and sprinkled and looked up at Shirley as if Shirley were the most important human in the world. Pretending to be Huguette, Shirley kissed the air on both sides of Natalie's face, ending with a kiss to the top of her nose.

Then, as Huguette liked to tell everyone but did not mean, Shirley told Natalie: *"Je t'aime!"* (French for "I love you"—say: "zhe tem"). But Shirley did mean it. The only thing Shirley loved about Huguette was the sound of her French, but her accent sounded no better than Mrs. Greif's even though Mrs. Greif was from Queens. Shirley smiled as she walked back up the hill with Natalie.

When Shirley opened the door to Aunt Claire's house, Aunt Claire, hands on hips, asked, "So did Natalie do her big business?"

Shirley turned radish red and said nothing.

Aunt Claire did an about-face and marched into the kitchen, muttering, "I'll be walking that dog at midnight."

When Pippi Longstocking lied, Shirley recalled, she said she was allowed to because her mother was an angel and her father was lost at sea. *My mother is not an angel,* Shirley thought, *but my father is kind of lost at sea, so maybe I could have half lied.* But she knew she couldn't have. Not in this lifetime.

Aunt Rosalie led the discussion at the dinner table with talk about the Barretts' upcoming trip to Lake Winnipesaukee. "Rod has his usual two-week vacation starting in the middle of July," she said, her long, dangling earrings swinging back and forth. "We'll be staying in a cabin at the Happy Hacienda again, which we were fortunate to get for the same price as last year because the place still has the same drippy faucets and leaky roof."

Aunt Rosalie laughed like a cartoon hyena: the *haha-has* had no spaces between them.

"We can't wait!" Aunt Rosalie told everyone. "The car is scheduled for a tune-up in a couple of weeks, and the kids will get their short summer haircuts after school is over."

Uncle Rod smiled at whatever Aunt Rosalie said. Shirley recognized that she and Uncle Rod were kindred spirits, content to be flies on the wall in any situation. If it weren't for Uncle Rod, Shirley knew she would never have been to just about every place she'd been to in her entire life: the Bronx Zoo, Rockaway Beach, Montauk, Bear Mountain State Park, and scores of Howard Johnson restaurants up and down the Bronx River and Sawmill River Parkways. That was because Shirley and Anna and Grandma always had standing—or sitting—invitations to go on day trips with the Barretts.

Uncle Rod waved his fingers in Shirley's direction as if to say, How about this year you finally come with us to Winnipesaukee?

It's at the top of my list, Shirley wanted to tell him, but she merely waved back.

"I want to go there now!" yelled Scott, sitting high in his seat thanks to two fat New York City telephone books.

"Who asked you?" said Aunt Rosalie like she always did whenever a kid proposed something that she herself didn't think of, or asked a question she didn't feel like answering.

The four other Barrett kids, Phillie included, enthusiastically agreed. "Yeah! Yeah! Yeah! Yeah!"

"Who asked you, too?" said Aunt Rosalie, getting happy giggles from each of her offspring because they knew their mother was only kidding.

But instead of feeling scared that Aunt Rosalie might challenge her if she asked to go, too, Shirley sat upright, surprising herself. *This may be my last chance,* she thought, looking at Uncle Rod and feeling that maybe she could do this after all. Shirley pictured the Smile of the Great Spirit as clear as day, beaming down on her all the way from Lake Winnipesaukee, drawing her toward the glorious mountains of New Hampshire.

"Speak up now, Shirley Burns!" a voice said in her head.

Shirley rotated the blue handball in her pocket six times for luck. But by the time she opened her mouth to speak, Aunt Claire had changed the subject to the upcoming wedding of her older daughter, Arlene. Flowers and music and dresses and guests. Blah. Blah. Blah. And Shirley completely lost her nerve.

Shirley's seat was next to Phillie's like it was every

Saturday. There was meatloaf tonight with a layer of mashed potatoes, hardboiled egg, and bacon in the middle. Phillie was left-handed and Shirley was right-handed, so she had to be careful not to let her elbow touch Phillie's elbow. Usually when they bumped funny bones, they would laugh uncontrollably. *There will be no laughing tonight,* Shirley predicted as if she were the weather person on TV.

"Ready for my bacon?" Phillie whispered, knowing how much Shirley detested any kind of eggs.

Normally, she would be happy to trade for Phillie's bacon. But not tonight. "No," she said.

Phillie wrinkled his eyebrows. "Who peed in your cornflakes?" he asked.

"You," Shirley answered, looking down at her plate as she picked out every last bit of egg and pushed it to the side.

"When?" Phillie asked.

Shirley didn't answer.

When it was time for dessert, Phillie tried to talk to her again. "Don't drink the milk," he said, clearly hoping Shirley would ask "Why?" the way she always did whenever they ate together. It was from a comedy routine they knew by heart from watching every single episode of the hilarious *Little Rascals* show on TV. But not this time.

"Shut up," Shirley said instead.

So Phillie, ready and eager to spout the usual warning—"Because it's spoiled"—was forced to keep the humor to himself.

Then without saying another word to the other, both cousins enjoyed generous slices of pineapple upside-down cake, Aunt Claire's specialty, along with milk in fancy crystal glasses. Shirley often wondered how Anna, having a sister like Aunt Claire, who made everything taste delicious and look so pretty you thought you were eating in a restaurant, could scarcely boil water.

When dinner was done and all that was left was grown-up talk, the kids, with the exception of Laurel and Ruthie and Esther and Arlene, who were at different stages of teenagerhood and liked to listen to the gossip, all left the table. Shirley slipped outside through the basement door, hoping no one (namely Phillie) would notice.

She stood in the driveway, pulled the blue ball from her pocket, and started throwing it against the brick wall of Aunt Claire's attached house. Throw-catch, throw-catch, throw-catch.

But then Phillie, who had been watching from behind the neighbor's bushes and trying his best to respect Shirley's bad mood and her silence for as long as he could, sprang out. Playfully attempting to steal the ball, he shouted, "Boo!"

Shirley merely said, "Thanks a lot for not telling me that I have no father when you knew all along that I didn't, traitor." Then she added, "Some best friend you are."

"How do *you* know I know?" Phillie asked, acting as if he didn't.

"You told me Aunt Rosalie thought I was a poor girl," said Shirley. "Why else would you say that?"

"The thing is, no one knows I know," said Phillie, rubbing the wart on his left hand, a thing he did whenever he was uneasy about something. "I overheard Grandma and my mom talking once about how sad it was that your dad died of a broken heart in a taxi. And how your mom didn't want you to know because you were only a little kid."

Shirley said, "I am not your best friend anymore, Phillip Barrett. Best friends tell each other everything. Especially important, life-affecting things like 'Your father is dead, Shirley Burns. You can stop hoping that he is ever coming back, starting now.' What was so hard about that? Kindly inform my mother that I have gone home."

Before Phillie could answer, Shirley turned on her heels and started walking past Aunt Claire's down-the-street neighbors: Helen Katz, sitting inside her fancy air-conditioned glass porch amid bags of hand-me-down clothes intended for people like Shirley (and Phillie, who also wore undershirts that said HELEN KATZ even though he was a boy); Freddie Reese, posing like an actor atop the new motorcycle in his driveway; and Mrs. Septimist, whose name Grandma could never pronounce correctly, rocking in one of those metal porch chairs.

Shirley skillfully bounced her ball on the sidewalk as she made her way back to Sparrowood Gardens, taking care not to let the ball hit a crack or a stone that would cause it to fly out of her reach and into the street.

Because Anna and Grandma were still at Aunt Claire's and the Sparrowood Gardens rental office was closed, Shirley had to find Luke to unlock their door with his master key. She was a little afraid that Luke might not be home. Then what would she do? Luke's apartment was in the basement next to the laundry room.

"Hey, Luke!" Shirley shouted through the open window. "Hey, Luke! Hey, Luuuuuuke!"

"What can I do for ye, missy?" Luke finally answered in his familiar, kind voice with the Scottish accent.

After Shirley explained, Luke accompanied her to her apartment, where he opened the door and waited in the hallway while Shirley switched on the lamp in the living room.

"Will ye be okay now, missy?" Luke asked. When Shirley said she would, he added, "Good night to ye, then."

"Thanks for everything, Luke," Shirley said. "Good night."

. . . . .

As she brushed her teeth, Shirley thought about Grandma's accent, so different from Luke's. *When I grow up,* she decided, *I will learn more Russian at a school where a perfect teacher like Mrs. Greif will be nice to me if I try hard.*

Shirley settled into bed with *Pippi Longstocking* and soon heard the click of the key in the lock telling her that Anna and Grandma were home from Aunt Claire's. Her heavy eyelids closed.

When Anna came into their bedroom to check on Shirley, she turned off the lamp, pulled the venetian blinds closed, returned *Pippi Longstocking* to Shirley's bedside table, and kissed her cheek. "Good night," Anna whispered. "Iloveyou."

I love you, too, Shirley thought, but was too tired to say.

Then Anna took her own nonlibrary book to the bathroom, where the bright overhead light allowed her to read without disturbing Grandma or Shirley while they slept.

Chapter 7
MINDING EVERYBODY'S
BUSINESS

THE SUN HAD BARELY RISEN OVER SPARROWOOD GARDENS WHEN Hurricane Anna began whipping from room to room collecting the past week's dirty laundry. She wanted to be first in line to nab two working washing machines before it got to be as busy as Grand Central Station down in the laundry room.

Grandma used to do their laundry on Thursdays, but she'd gotten fired the previous week for turning Anna's favorite white blouse pink when she forgot to remove her own flowery red underpants from the light-colored wash.

"Let's go, Shirley! No time for dawdling," Anna yelled from the doorway of the bedroom. "Hurry up and get dressed! We have a lot of work to do. Remember, it's Father's Day, too. When it rains, it pours."

Shirley knew that Anna was referring not to the

weather, but to the number of things that had to be accomplished before dinnertime, when her friend Hal would arrive. She wondered if Anna would make her give Hal a Father's Day card.

"I'm glad it's sunny," said Anna, "so we can hang out."

Shirley figured that *hanging out* had everything to do with laundry and nothing to do with hanging around shooting the breeze in what little breeze there was today, if any.

Anna stripped the beds and gathered the towels, washcloths, underwear, blouses, socks, pajamas, shorts, and dresses.

"Can you lend me some quarters?" she asked Shirley. "I don't have any change."

Shirley complied. Then she watched as Anna, in a frenzied fit, looked down at her watch to assure herself that she would be first when Luke unlocked the laundry room door at eight.

Shirley, still in her pajamas, sighed as she stared out the window at the playground beyond the big crab-apple tree. There were two squeaky green seesaws, four swings (one with a dangerously dangling crooked seat, another that gave you splinters on your rear right through your pants, all with rusty chains), and the long metal slide that burned your thighs if you were dumb enough to slide down in the heat of a late afternoon in shorts.

Shirley saw Mrs. Goodman and her little boy, Markie, already outside on this stifling early-summer morning, digging in the same sandbox that Shirley had once seen Monica Callahan pee in when she couldn't be bothered going home to do it.

Shirley changed into her clothes and wondered why she needed to go with Anna to the laundry room. But not for long.

When they arrived, they discovered that Mrs. Goodman had actually been there first—Markie's bedsheets, cloth diapers, and baby clothes were swishing around in the best machine. Apparently, Luke sometimes opened the laundry room early on Sundays without asking Anna's permission.

"Watch closely, Shirley," said Anna as she began to scrub the inside of another machine in an effort to eliminate every germ known to womankind using a holey undershirt that had once belonged to Helen Katz. "Here." Anna handed Shirley another well-worn Helen Katz undershirt so Shirley could perform the identical scrubbing technique on another washing machine. Once they were done, Anna dumped their whites into one machine, the darks in the other, and said, "I want you to stay down here until the machines stop spinning to make sure no one takes out our clean wash with their dirty hands and puts it on the dirty table."

Anna's chin pointed first to the square Formica table that had a stray blue sock on it, along with a wad of reddish lint and a partially sucked-on purple lollipop, and then to the long, hard wooden bench, newly painted apartment-green, where Shirley was to sit while she waited.

Her mother was treating her like a grown-up for once in her life. None of the other kids Shirley's age ever came near the laundry room except to roller-skate. Or to play spin the bottle.

"Doing the laundry is not to be taken lightly, you know," said Anna, continuing to explain the newly assigned Sunday duty to Shirley. "When the machines stop spinning, please put the wet laundry in the basket and carry it to the clothesline. I will meet you there in exactly twenty-eight minutes to show you the right way to hang it. There is just enough time between now and then for me to clean the bathroom for tonight—and to have a cup of coffee and a cigarette."

When Mrs. Goodman and Markie came back into the laundry room, Shirley politely said hi. She liked Mrs. Goodman, and she loved Markie as much as she loved all babies.

Shirley blew Markie's pinwheel around, making him laugh, while Mrs. Goodman transferred her wet laundry to the dryer. Shirley guessed Mrs. Goodman wasn't hanging her wash outside because it was too hard to keep an eye on Markie at the same time. Shirley knew her mother didn't approve of her babysitting ("We don't do those kinds of things, Shirley"), so Shirley didn't offer to watch Markie now, even though she would have loved to chase him around the playground.

"Anytime you are ready to babysit," Mrs. Goodman told her again, "I would gladly pay you the going rate. You are a very responsible girl, Shirley—and Markie adores you."

What is my problem? Shirley asked herself. *Why can't I just tell Anna that I am going to babysit? She can call Mrs. Goodman's house whenever she wants to see that I am still alive.*

Grandma's friend Augusta came into the laundry room and dumped her wash into the last empty machine. "Say hiya to your grandma for me, okay?" she said as she was leaving.

"I will," said Shirley.

When Mrs. Goodman took Markie outside to play on the swings, Shirley sat on the bench and listened to a washing machine rinsing, leaking water from its rusty bottom out onto the floor—*drip, drip, drip*—and to the metal buttons of Markie's overalls clinking against the sides of the dryer—*clink, clink, clink.*

The belowground laundry room, usually the best place

to be on a humid summer day, felt unbearably hot all of a sudden: hot water, hot pipes, hot motors, hot dryer drums, hot air wafting in from outside. It was so hard-to-breathe hot that Shirley had to fan away the sweat on her face with her hand.

Shirley's eyes landed on the purple lollipop. She got up and threw it into the trash can, thinking Markie might try to suck on it. She sat back down and nervously played with a cuticle on her thumb until it bled. Then she licked it. *Gross,* she thought. She swung her Keds back and forth underneath the bench, wishing she'd brought a book, and checked her watch to find that barely two minutes had gone by, then three minutes when she heard someone shout.

"Hey, Shirley! Grandma told me you'd be down here. Look what I have!" The kickstand of Phillie's bike scraped the cement floor as he swung his leg around and splashed his black high-top Converse sneakers into a puddle of suds.

Shirley's heart thumped. Not because she was startled at the interruption, but because she was actually happy to see Phillie. In spite of herself.

"Oh, it's you," she said, trying to sound mad, because she still was. But she was also interested to see what Phillie had. She noticed he was wearing a blue polo shirt with all the Barrett kids' names printed in a continuing unbroken line across the front:

LAURELRUTHIESTEVEPHILLIESCOTTLAURELRUTH-
IESTEVEPHILLIESCOTTLAURELRUTHIESTEVEPHIL-
LIESCOTTLAURELRUTHIESTEVEPHILLIESCOTTLAUREL-
RUTHIESTEVEPHILLIESCOTT

Of course, there was no SHIRLEY, even though she always pictured her name there in the age-appropriate spot—after the STEVE and before the PHILLIE. Uncle Rod had made the shirts at his printing job.

Phillie reached into the left pocket of his shorts and pulled out some bubble-gum cigars—one pink, one yellow, and one mint green—that Shirley knew he'd received as part of his pay from working at Red's Variety Store that morning, compiling sections of weekend newspapers: the *New York Times,* the *New York Post,* the *Daily News,* and the *Mirror.*

"Ta-da!" Phillie said with a flourish, holding the gum in front of Shirley's nose so she could smell the enticing, artificially delicious flavors right through the wrappers. Then, sensing a slight change in his cousin and best friend's attitude, Phillie pulled out a thick wad of dollar bills from his back pocket. "My stash of cash," he told her.

Phillie was a saver, too.

Phillie and I are so much alike, Shirley thought. The difference between them was their mothers: Anna, who wouldn't let Shirley make any money babysitting, and

Aunt Rosalie, who had so many kids that she couldn't keep track of each one every second. So many that Phillie could go around his neighborhood asking people if he could paint their houses, shovel their snow, rake their leaves, or even trim their trees because Phillie wasn't afraid of climbing high up on a ladder. All at the ripe old age of eleven—just three months younger than Shirley, to be exact—without anyone ever telling him that he needed to be safe at home. Phillie even had a business. It was called Barrett Enterprises.

"I'm saving for an Aurora Road Race set, and I'm almost there," Phillie announced. "You can help me pick it out."

Shirley made herself look away.

But Phillie didn't give up so easily. "I made a table for it in the basement right near Harry's fishbowl so he can watch the cars go around the track. I want to buy it before we go to Lake Winnipesaukee. Hey, Shirley, are you listening?"

Shirley didn't answer.

Next Phillie said, "Want to go to the park and play tennis? We can chew gum and blow bubbles while we ride our bikes there. See? I brought my tennis racket. I'll even let you beat me." Phillie pointed to the space behind the seat of his bike where the racket was wedged in. "And," he added, rubbing the wart on his left hand, "I should have told you about your father. I'm really sorry. Cross my heart and hope to die." Phillie made a big X with his pointer finger close to the middle of his LAURELRUTHIESTEVEPHILLIESCOTT shirt.

"Don't let it happen again," said Shirley. She could never stay mad at Phillie for very long.

Shirley reached for the yellow bubble-gum cigar because it tasted like banana, her favorite. Fortunately, Phillie liked everything green, so there was no argument. He put the pink cigar back in his pocket for later, along with his money. Shirley smiled. She bit off the top of the yellow cigar and savored the taste of fake banana. Phillie, on the other hand, put the entire cigar between his lips as if it were real. Shirley would have none of that real-cigar stuff because of Hal.

"Thanks," she told Phillie, "but I can't go yet because my mother told me that I have to hang out the wash this morning since Grandma is not doing it anymore."

The washing machines stopped. Shirley carefully pulled their laundry out and into the waiting plastic basket.

When Hurricane Anna came whipping around the doorway, Shirley quickly pushed the rest of the banana bubble-gum cigar into her back pocket and swallowed the piece in her mouth. But not quickly enough.

"Are you eating candy before breakfast?" Anna asked. Then, "Why weren't you at the clothesline, Shirley?" To

Phillie, she said, "Hi, Phillie. You can have breakfast with us after we're done."

"Okay, Aunt Anna," Phillie said cheerfully. He wheeled his bike up the ramp of the laundry room behind Anna and Shirley, then headed to the playground, where he could watch them.

Shirley knew he wouldn't mess with Hurricane Anna for all the bubble gum in Canada, which was where the cigars were made.

First, Anna wrapped an old washcloth around the clothesline and held on to it as she walked from one end of the metal post to the other; then she walked back again for good measure.

"Look at this filth," Anna said, unfurling the washcloth to reveal a black, ropelike impression of dirt. "Now you do it."

Shirley, who could barely reach the top of the clothesline, walked on tiptoes from one end of a different line to the other and back again for good measure. She opened the washcloth to reveal the dirt she'd wiped off.

"See?" said Anna.

Shirley beamed. Compliments from her mother, even offhanded ones, were hard to come by.

Anna continued, "Shake everything out first, Shirley. Don't let the sheets or towels touch the ground, even for an instant; hang the blouses by their collars, the shorts and Grandma's underpants by their waists, the socks by their tops so the foot parts are sure to dry; don't fold the pillowcases over the top of the clothesline, because then you'll have to put your face on a deep wrinkle which, in turn, will give your cheeks deep wrinkles when you wake up. Dresses get hung by their shoulders."

As if the laundry were people, Shirley thought.

"I don't iron sheets, pillowcases, or your grandmother's hankies," Anna rattled on. "I do iron blouses and dresses, but I won't have to if you hang them up right the first time."

Anna watched while Shirley hung. She made Shirley start again when a pair of shorts wasn't pinned just right. Anna didn't use the straight wooden kind of clothespin that could pop off and allow the clean sheets to drag along the ground. She preferred the more reliable plastic kind that came in all colors and had a spring that kept snapping shut on Shirley's fingers.

Shirley could see Phillie swinging on one of the good swings in the playground. He was going so high that the chains on either side of the swing lost their tautness and Phillie's feet almost touched the top of the thick steel bar from which the swings swung. The hanging out couldn't be over fast enough.

Finally Anna gave her approval.

"Phillie, I'm done!" Shirley called.

But Anna wasn't. Not quite. "I'm taking the basket

home with me, Shirley, so no one will steal it and so it won't get dusty or soiled by a pigeon before you need it again this afternoon, when you will please take the dry wash off the lines, fold it all neatly, and put each clothes-pin back in the clothespin bag." Then she relented a little. "Grandma is making breakfast, so you and Phillie should come inside soon."

Shirley joined Phillie, swinging on the other good swing. She didn't go nearly as high as he did and instead let the back-and-forth motion of the swing calm her. Shir-ley preferred her feet on the ground or as close to the ground as possible. When they'd had enough, they went to Shirley's apartment for breakfast: French toast made just how they liked it—crisp not soggy, topped with Grandma's apricot jam.

"I'm glad you like it," said Grandma, wiping her hands on her apron.

Anna was already ironing a special tablecloth in prep-aration for Hal's visit.

Shirley then retrieved her bike and tennis racket from the bedroom. She checked her pocket for the ball. It was there.

"And by the way, Phillie, there is no way on earth that I need you to let me beat you. I can wallop you with my eyes closed," Shirley said as she maneuvered her bike outside to where Phillie had parked his.

Phillie smiled.

Shirley flew with him down the steep hill directly to Park Drive, her tennis racket secured under her right arm. There wasn't much traffic on Sunday, so Shirley and Phillie rode in the street. They blew giant bubbles like champions—bubbles that popped in the air and not all over their faces.

"When's your last day of school?" asked Phillie, who went to a different public school in his neighborhood.

"Same as yours," Shirley answered. "I don't go to school in Milwaukee, you know. New York City schools are all the same, unless you go to Our Lady Queen of Peace or to reform school, which you should, because you withheld information from your best friend—and you need to reform for a crime like that."

"Hardy har har," said Phillie.

Chapter 8
SHIRLEY'S WINNING SMILE

SHIRLEY AND PHILLIE LEFT THEIR BIKES IN THE BIKE RACK AT THE park near the water fountain.

"Don't put your mouth on it," Phillie said, mimicking both his mother and Shirley's.

Shirley stuck her tongue out at Phillie. "Who asked you?" she said.

He stuck his tongue out at her and said, "I asked me."

"What would happen if I did put my mouth on the water spout?" she asked.

"Probably nothing," said Phillie. "Our mothers just like to tell us what to do."

They both laughed and spit their gum in the trash bin on their way to the court.

Then a fierce combination of tennis, squash, and handball ensued, Shirley and Phillie each smashing the high-bouncing blue ball against the cement wall with the wooden rackets they'd received under Phillie's tree last Christmas. Shirley loved her racket. It had a picture of Pancho Gonzales, the world-famous tennis player, on the neck just beneath the racket part. Phillie's racket once had Rod Laver on it, but because he had to share it with Steve and Scott, most of Rod's face had worn off.

Seventy minutes later, the last of three close, grueling games, made even more grueling by the unbearable heat and humidity, was nearly over. Phillie served his best serve. But Shirley was ready for it. She hauled her racket back, and then, with all her strength and determination, whacked the ball as low and as hard as she could, aiming for the inside of the singles line.

"Lucky!" shouted Phillie, dripping with sweat, as Shirley's ball grazed the cement of the court, sealing her win by the required two points.

"Couldn't have done it without Pancho," she said, smiling, as she headed for the water fountain.

"How about we trade rackets next time?" said Phillie.

"In your dreams," said Shirley.

They pedaled home side by side. As they rode through the shade underneath the overpass to the highway, Phillie said, "Reminds me of the day we rode to LaGuardia on our bikes and went under the belly, wings, and tail of that parked jet, and my bike chain came off and you fixed it, and no one even told us to get lost."

"During Easter vacation," said Shirley. "That was fun!"

Then Phillie said, "Speaking of fun, I just got new goggles for Lake Winnipesaukee, so I can open my eyes underwater. They had three colors at Wainwright's: red, green, and blue."

Before he had a chance to tell her, Shirley knew Phillie had picked green.

"I wish you could come," he added, looking her way. "We'd have the greatest time, but . . ."

"But what?" she asked.

"But your mother won't let you go. I heard my parents talking about it last night. My mother said"—here Phillie assumed his mother's voice—"'Shirley would adore Lake Winnipesaukee!'" Then Phillie said, "I didn't tell you before in the laundry room because I thought you might not feel like going to the park. You'd be too mad."

Shirley suddenly couldn't breathe. Her first impulse was to pretend she hadn't heard what Phillie said. To save face. Her face. To make light of the situation. She should have known all along that it was Anna who, every year, stood in Shirley's way to Lake Winnipesaukee like a roadblock, and not Aunt Rosalie wanting to keep the trip for her family only.

"I don't really care, Phillie," Shirley answered with a shaky laugh.

It's always Anna, Shirley thought. *Being ridiculous, being overly cautious, insisting on her Safe-at-Home Doctrine. Anna, who thought that not telling me that my father was dead was protecting me. Protecting me from the truth that I had a right to know. One day I will find a way to get her to see how mistaken she's been all these years, but right now it's hard for me to speak up.* Especially *to a hurricane.*

So Shirley changed the subject.

"Maybe we can give Hal the pink bubble-gum cigar," she said, "so he won't reek of real cigar."

"Are you kidding?" said Phillie. "No way!" And he broke the last bubble-gum cigar in half, handing Shirley her share while each of them continued riding.

With his mouth full of bubble gum, Phillie told a joke. "Hey, Shirl," he asked, "why do vampires need mouthwash?"

Shirley didn't answer.

Phillie filled the pause. "Because they have *bat* breath."

"Ha ha," Shirley said, not at all in the mood to laugh.

"Am I your boyfriend, Shirley?" Phillie asked.

"Phillie, you nut!" Shirley answered. "Cousins can't be boyfriend and girlfriend except in the case of Franklin D. Roosevelt and Eleanor. Besides, I already have a boyfriend."

"Who is it?" asked Phillie.

"A kid in my class named Maury," said Shirley, trying to sound casual. "He saves me a seat on the bus every day."

"I have a girlfriend, too," confessed Phillie. "Her name is Vivian. She brings green Lik-m-aid for me in her lunchbox. She's not as pretty as you, and she doesn't have eyes with yellow sunflowers in them like you. But she's still pretty."

"You lie like a rug," said Shirley.

"Remember we used to pretend we were husband and wife going to Florida in that old car in the abandoned lot across from my house?" Phillie asked. "It was a blue Olds with two doors and a ton of rust."

"Yeah," said Shirley. "You always hogged the steering wheel."

"Yeah," said Phillie. "Bet that was a really nice car before the mice ate the seats."

"Blech," said Shirley.

After that they rode in silence until Phillie had to turn right onto 75th Avenue, which would take him home to the fun and disorganized Barrett house while Shirley continued straight ahead to the mini museum that was not at all fun and way too organized.

"See ya, Shirl," Phillie said.

"See ya, Phil," said Shirley.

Chapter 9
THE MICKEY MOUSE CLUB SONG SUNG SADLY

LATER THAT SUNDAY AFTERNOON, BEHIND THE BIG BASKET OF meticulously folded laundry—towels on the bottom, pajamas next, followed by dresses, then underwear and socks, with shirts and shorts on top—Shirley walked through the clothesline area. She ducked under Maury's Boy Scout uniform, his father's mailman uniform along with six white shirts, Grandma's friend Augusta's big black brassieres and matching slips, Mr. Bickerstaff's hunting vests, and Luke's gray Sparrowood Gardens overalls with the pockets turned out like elephants' ears—and started home.

Shirley was thinking how absurd it was that she knew everyone's garments, outer and inner, when she suddenly heard Beryl Abbie singing a song from TV. The problem was that Shirley couldn't see Beryl Abbie over the big basket of laundry she was carrying.

"I went into the water, but I didn't get wet. I didn't get wet. I didn't get wet. I went into the water, but I didn't get wet. Yet."

"Watch out!" Shirley yelled. It wasn't that she was concerned that she was headed for certain smash-up with Beryl Abbie. It was more that Shirley had seen something on the ground that she was afraid Beryl Abbie might step on if she didn't alert her quickly and in a big way.

What Shirley saw was a mouse: an unexpectedly still, solitary, perfect mouse.

Shirley put the basket down in the grass to investigate, and then both girls bent over the little creature lying peacefully on his side. Shirley looked for signs of life in the mouse: a rise and fall in his tiny chest or a twitch of his whiskers. She thought for sure that he would run away. Shirley was a giant compared to the mouse. But there was no movement at all. It occurred to Shirley that he was the biggest dead thing she had ever been so close to.

"Wake up, Mouse," Shirley whispered, just in case her diagnosis was wrong. Gently, she prodded him with her finger, but the mouse fell back as he had lain before, fur still warm from being recently alive. He had tiny white teeth and tiny nails, pointy and sharp, and whiskers the color of bluish milk. His feet were longer than Shirley had imagined a mouse's feet would be, and there was a pink, wormlike tail at the end of his body. The mouse's fur was gray, with some brown mixed in. And he was soft.

"He's mine, Beryl Abbie," Shirley said, thinking, *So that's what it looks like when you're dead.*

"Oh," Beryl Abbie answered, readily accepting the fact that the mouse now belonged to Shirley. "Can I touch him, please?"

"Sure," said Shirley.

But then Beryl Abbie jumped back without touching him.

"There is nothing to be afraid of," Shirley said. "Being dead is not catching."

Then, using both hands, Shirley picked up the mouse as if he were one of Aunt Claire's fragile Saturday-night dinner glasses and placed him on the mountain of folded laundry as if he were a king. Anna's short shorts were on top and served as a pillow for the little body. Then Shirley and Beryl Abbie, who began singing a heartfelt hymn to the poor soul, walked toward Shirley's apartment. The dirge was actually the theme song from *The Mickey Mouse Club* on Channel 5. Shirley knew it well and joined in.

"M-I-C-K-E-Y M-O-U-S-E," they dolefully sang.

Then Beryl Abbie went her way and Shirley went hers.

When Shirley got to her stoop, she lifted the mouse and put him in the shade under Grandma's rambling rosebush.

"Wait here. I'll be right back," she told him, brushing some dirt off Anna's shorts before she opened the door to the apartment and went inside.

A few minutes later Shirley returned with an empty checkbook box. There was a picture of a globe on the outside over the words *See the World* in black letters. Shirley had made the inside of the box into a bed with cotton balls as soft as clouds, quite appropriate, she imagined, for a creature about to float upward on his way to heaven. Actually, Shirley wasn't sure what happened to dead things or how long it took to go wherever it was you went when you had no life left inside you to live. She was new to the whole dead thing.

Maybe being dead isn't so terrible, Shirley thought, studying the mouse. He looked as calm as if he were listening to music. The kind of soft, dandelion-puff music Madame Macaroni sometimes played on the old piano at ballet class when she wasn't pounding on it to get everyone's attention.

"Are you okay, Mouse?" Shirley asked as she settled him into his checkbook-box bed.

Shirley had written *This Mouse Belongs to Shirley* on the inside of the lid because it was painfully sad to think that he belonged to no one. *Born: 3/6* (her father's birthday) *Died: 6/18.*

"I might not tell Phillie about you, Mouse, although he specializes in small animals. Case in point: Harry the piranha, who follows Phillie's pencil by swimming back and forth when Phillie does his homework. That is, if Phillie does his homework." Phillie was not what Shirley would call an especially studious student. "I might not even tell Grandma, who is still the smartest person I know."

And she certainly wasn't going to tell Anna, who would insist that Shirley immediately flush the dead mouse down the toilet.

"No one would understand about you, Mouse," Shirley said. "By the way, I have decided to make you my father in honor of Father's Day. To keep you near me. So I will always know where to find you, like other kids always know where to find their fathers. Isn't it better to have a dead mouse for a father than no father at all?"

When Shirley returned inside, Anna said, "Here's the card for Hal, Shirley. Aren't the sailboats and the palm trees dreamy? He'll love the 'Dear Big Daddy' you're going to write at the top, too."

Shirley did not want Hal for her father, but she wrote *Dear Big Daddy* anyway.

I will never say those words out loud, she thought. *Not ever. I have a father now. Even if he's a make-believe one under Grandma's rosebush.*

Chapter 10
YCDBSOYA

"HIYA, SKINNY," HAL SAID WHEN SHIRLEY LET HIM INTO THEIR apartment.

Shirley wanted to tell Hal to shut up. But she couldn't utter a single word. Not even *hi*. She took as deep a breath as she could and stepped aside to make way for Hal. Then to avoid what was coming next, Shirley kept her head down. But it came anyway after Hal removed the straw hat from his mostly hairless head and placed it on the ceramic head of Bambi sitting on top of the big console TV.

Hal then puckered up his slimy lips (his rust-colored brush of a mustache included), placed them on Shirley's cheek, and left them there for what seemed like an hour. Shirley recoiled in disgust, but the recoil was not so obvious that Anna could object and make Shirley go back for another one of Hal's kisses. A do-over. Shirley wished Hal would kiss the air around her like Aunt Claire's friend Huguette did.

"Hal loves you so much," Anna whispered in Shirley's ear.

But Shirley couldn't stop saying *gross* to herself, over and over.

"You grew some," Hal said, lifting Shirley's chin with his hand. Hal liked to play with words to impress Anna, who always thought he was so funny.

Shirley did not appreciate Hal's *gruesome* humor.

When Hal leaned over to kiss Grandma hello, Grandma skillfully avoided him by rearranging the roses that didn't need rearranging in the vase on the dinette table.

Hal had presents for everyone. The pair of summer sandals for Shirley squeezed her pinkie toes as soon as she slid her feet in, but she didn't dare complain to Hal for fear of incurring Anna's wrath. To Grandma, he offered a pair of old-lady sandals, which Grandma, as usual, would not accept, whether or not she liked them.

"Look!" Grandma said, pointing to her feet. "I just got these snazzy sandals last veek from Macy's. Vhy do I need another pair?"

Shirley knew Grandma didn't like anything old-ladyish, not to mention anything Hal-ish either.

"That man is a vorld-class lying snake in the grass,"

Grandma had told Anna when Hal, whom Anna had known back when she was sixteen, had started showing up a few years ago at their apartment after he'd found Anna again in the phone book.

Anna had informed Grandma that she had better stick to her knitting or there would be big trouble.

After refusing the old-lady sandals, Grandma said nothing further to Hal, although Anna was waiting expectantly. Shirley knew that Hurricane Anna would not embarrass Grandma in front of Hal the way she would embarrass Shirley, because Grandma was a strong hurricane, too.

"I vill put borscht on your head if you do," Grandma had once warned.

"That was so nice of you, Hal," said Anna, modeling the new navy-blue pumps that looked to Shirley like a serious fashion statement along with Anna's short shorts.

Hal sat down on Grandma's bed, which was dressed up as the couch. He bit off a minuscule piece of cigar and spit it into the air. *"Ptwo."* Then quite methodically, he struck a match, lit the cigar, and rolled the bitten-off end around in his mouth, sending putrid puffs up to the ceiling and out the window like smoke signals.

Shirley watched as he sauntered over to the special Hal cabinet in their one-person-at-a-time kitchen to pour "the usual" as if he had been living with Anna, Grandma, and Shirley for years and did this every night after work.

Shirley narrowed her eyes. *Don't get any ideas, Hal,* she told him silently. *This is not your home. And it never will be.* Shirley thought of Mouse and stood up taller.

"Would you care for a drink, Annie?" Hal asked Anna.

Anna didn't usually care for a drink, but she cared for one today. "Thank you, love," Anna said, receiving her drink and sipping it while she straightened the tie clip on Hal's shirt with her other hand.

Shirley and Grandma rolled their eyes at the same time.

"I'm really hungry," Shirley whispered to Grandma.

So Grandma said, "Okay, my sunny child. In vone second."

Shirley sat next to Hal and across from Anna at the small dinette table. Shirley had put the cracked plate, the dullest knife, and the cloth napkin with the permanent spaghetti-sauce stain at Hal's place like she did every Sunday when she set the table, hoping he wouldn't come back. But he always did.

Shirley suspected that Hal knew Grandma didn't like him, even though Grandma was careful to say her favorite unflattering things about him under her breath in Russian, like "Go fly a kite," which when translated literally meant "Go hang yourself up," as if Hal were a shirt, a telephone receiver, or an oil painting from Mr. Joseph's.

When Grandma arrived with the first course, baked whitefish with tomatoes and lemon slices and homemade rye bread, Hal stood up to display his good manners— which made his napkin slide off his lap and onto the floor. Then as he bent over to pick it up, a series of deafening motorcycle-like noises issued from behind him.

Now in her chair across from Hal, Grandma said, "Pew!" She coughed subtly and turned her head sideways to hide her disgust, too polite to do anything more drastic, because, after all, Hal was their guest.

Shirley couldn't stop her mouth from dropping open in disbelief. *If I ever did that,* she thought, *Anna would banish me from the dinner table in two wags of a dog's tail.*

Anna, who was now delicately placing her own napkin in her lap, tried to look as if nothing had happened.

Shirley did not look at Hal while he was relating the events of his very busy day, which had started at the crack of dawn: shoes in a shoe store here, shoes in a shoe store there, a yellow polka-dot bikini on one mannequin, a muu-muu on another.

"I have keys to hundreds of stores, so I can work anytime I want," Hal boasted. "Even on Sundays."

However, when Hal noticed that Shirley wasn't paying

attention, he let his fork fall with such drama that she was certain his cracked plate would shatter to pieces.

"I'm tawkin' to ya," Hal said, glaring at Shirley as if she had just committed the crime of a lifetime.

Shirley immediately looked up, fuchsia-faced, stomach rising and falling like a roller coaster, and realized that she was scared of him. *Except when I'm in the Palace of Light, where I'm not afraid of anything or anyone,* she thought. Shirley longed to go there right this second. She would take Mouse with her and never come out when Hal was around. Shirley could not bring herself to look at Hal as he continued his shoe stories. So she stared at his tie clip, sensing that the storm had passed without further incident.

To keep his fancy silk tie out of Grandma's Sunday dinners, Hal always wore a metal tie clip with the engraved letters *YCDBSOYA*. For the longest time, Shirley had tried to figure out what the letters stood for. But because she would only talk to Hal when it was absolutely necessary or when Anna was closely monitoring, Shirley could only guess. Today's attempt was *Yaks Can Die By Swallowing Oily Yellow Ants.*

Along with the shoes for Grandma, Anna, and Shirley, Hal had brought a new word, like he did every Sunday, a word that he had heard during the week whose meaning he did not know. Usually Shirley had never heard of the word and forgot it as soon as Hal said it. However, last week's word, *largesse*, had stuck with her because it sounded French. As explained by Anna, it meant "generosity."

Shirley was now only slightly starving, having nibbled on some bread. She did not eat the fish because it had too many bones and too many eyes. The second course was going to be cucumber salad with Grandma's yogurt and fresh dill, which Shirley loved. But the rule was that Grandma could not serve it until after the word challenge was over. Shirley's stomach rumbled as she waited.

"Mandacious," announced Hal with authority.

Who cares? Shirley thought.

"Go to the devil's mother," mumbled Grandma in Russian.

At first Shirley thought Hal had succeeded in impressing Anna. She seemed to love the word. But then Shirley could tell that Anna had something up her sleeve.

"First of all, Hal," said Anna, mixing sweetness with smugness, "the word is *MENdacious*, not *MANdacious*."

Hal opened his eyes wide with admiration.

Anna, who liked to show off, too, was just warming up. *"Mendacious* is characteristic of someone who lies," she said. Because Anna read so much in the bathroom at night, she knew a lot of big words.

Hal applauded, while opposite him, Grandma concentrated on wiping the humidity off her eyeglasses and Shirley concentrated on the *YCDBSOYA* on Hal's tie clip. She stifled a yawn so that Hal would not drop his fork again. But she couldn't stifle several sneezes, which made Anna leave her chair and remove the vase of roses to the kitchen. *It won't matter,* Shirley told herself, *because it is Hal that I am allergic to, not the roses.*

Seizing the opportunity to escape for a few minutes while Anna and Hal only had eyes for each other, Shirley slipped off her seat. "I'll be back in time for the second course," she said, glad when no one answered. Shirley placed the Big Daddy Father's Day card to the right of Hal's elbow next to a small white box labeled *For Hal* in peacock blue, the contents undoubtedly obtained by Anna on layaway at Mr. Joseph's.

I do not want to be here when Hal opens that card, Shirley told herself. *He will stare at me for six thousand seconds just to show Anna how profoundly touched he is by what she made me write.* Shirley was careful not to let the screen door bang.

"I don't like Hal," Shirley told Mouse under the rosebush. "And you wouldn't either. Anna makes me include him in my prayers: God bless Anna, Hal, Grandma, Aunt Rosalie, Uncle Rod, Laurel, Ruthie, Steve, Phillie, Scott,

Aunt Claire, Uncle Bill, Arlene, and Esther. But tonight, Mouse, I'm going to replace Hal's name with yours."

When Shirley came back inside, Grandma had brought out the cucumber salad.

"This tastes like nectar from the gods," Hal told Grandma.

That was another untruth because nectar was sweet and yogurt was sour. Shirley played with some toothpicks that Anna had placed in a ramekin next to Hal so he could clean his teeth at the table, which he liked to do even though Shirley and Grandma thought it was totally disgusting.

Hal waited until after dessert—Grandma's oozy peach pie with hot and sugary Lipton tea in glasses the way real Russians drank their tea—to open the card and present. It was a new silver money clip.

Hal began to relight his cigar while Anna began to relate the minutiae of that long-ago day when they had first met as teenagers. "It's fate that brought us together again, don't you think?" Anna cooed.

Grandma clicked her spoon around in her glass. Then she made especially loud sipping noises. Finally she said, "I need to get out of here," in Russian, standing and pushing her chair away.

Shirley smiled as she fiddled with the toothpicks, having nothing better to do till dinner was over.

After a few minutes, Shirley thought she heard Hal say, "Shoiley, what do you think?"

So she looked up. Hal looked down.

The word ALLOWANCE had been spelled out in front of Shirley on the tablecloth with twenty-eight toothpicks.

Shirley waited to get kicked under the table by Anna for being a smart aleck. She quickly pulled her sandaled feet with their squeezed pinkie toes under her chair just in case. But no kick came. The calm before another storm, Shirley figured.

Hal removed the cigar from his mouth. He placed it in the Mr. Joseph ashtray, which Anna had brought to the table. He stared at Shirley for six thousand seconds. He peeled pie dough from his fingers. He wiped peaches from his rusty mustache. He took a sip of sweet tea. He swallowed. Hal's bloodshot blue eyes never left Shirley's eyes. His face turned to stone. Then, in an unexpected turn, Hal exploded into thunderous guffaws.

Hal's unusually pale head turned hot pink, the gold teeth all the way in the back showed out of his mouth, and Shirley could see his entire tongue for the first time ever. Hal's nose ran; his eyes ran. The dishes and glasses shook on the table along with Hal's jowls. When he leaned forward to get closer to Shirley, familiar shots rang out from somewhere between the seat of Hal's pants and the seat of his seat.

Shirley did not know what to make of the situation—until Anna, no longer able to contain herself, burst out laughing, too. Grandma appeared from the kitchen to see what all the commotion was about. She didn't even crack a smile.

Shirley did, but only after Hal reached into his pocket and pulled out two crisp one-dollar bills.

"Thanks," said Shirley.

After that, Hal was in such good humor that he helped clear the table. But when he carried the dishes to the kitchen and put them on the counter, he hit his head on the corner of a cabinet door Anna had left open when she'd brought out the jade ashtray for Hal's cigar.

"Oh, Hal, I'm so sorry," said Anna at the sight of the Red Sea on Hal's head.

Anna stood there apologizing over and over like a broken record until Grandma had to tell her to stop, in Russian, of course, so Hal wouldn't understand because Grandma had just called Anna a cow.

Then Shirley ran to the Palace of Light for a Band-Aid to stick on Hal's wound. And Hal, seeing stars, stuck his cigar lips on Shirley's cheek, this time to express his gratitude for her quick and practical thinking.

Don't get any ideas, Hal, Shirley thought. *It was the only thing I could do since my mother is a bubblehead. I still do not want you for my father.*

At twenty past six, Hal announced that he had to leave. "I would love to stay longer. You know you are my three most favorite girls, but You Can't Do Business Sitting On Your Ass. So I have to get going."

To which Grandma replied, "Vat took you so long?" under the running water in the kitchen sink.

To which Shirley thought, *So that's what it means,* beginning to unbuckle her new sandals.

To which Anna complained, "So soon?" as her lips met Hal's, sounding more like a plunger, to Shirley, than a kiss.

After Hal left, Anna dried the dishes, pots, and utensils that Grandma had just washed and Shirley turned her new shoebox into a diorama. She got some paper and drew a perfectly detailed Anna, Grandma, Shirley, and Hal; cut them out; and placed them around a paper table on paper chairs that she bent and attached to the floor of the shoebox with Magic tape. She then pasted paper pies that she colored Crayola peach to everyone's paper plate except Hal's. He got a paper mouse. As soon as Paper Hal realized there was a mouse on his plate, he jumped up, with Shirley's help, tearing his paper self and his paper chair. With Shirley's help also, a frantic Paper Anna shrieked, "Shirley, get this monster out of here!" Shirley laughed. Did Paper Anna mean Hal or the mouse?

Chapter 11
DIGGING DOWN DEEP

IT WAS WARM AND BUGGY AND STILL PRETTY LIGHT OUT WHEN,
dishes done, food packed away, TV turned on for *The Ed
Sullivan Show* at eight, Shirley went back outside. There
would be no Big Daddy card till next Father's Day. Shirley
heard Mr. Bickerstaff's venetian blinds rattle upstairs
and saw Mustard's face between the slats. "It's only me,"
she said. Mustard stood ready to protect Mr. Bickerstaff
from all harm. But he didn't bark because, no doubt, he'd
recognized Shirley's voice. Needless to say, Shirley was
quite happy to have what was left of the day and Mouse
all to herself.

"I finally know that *YCDBSOYA* means 'You Can't Do
Business Sitting On Your Ass,'" Shirley told Mouse after
she lifted the top of the checkbook box. "I hate to admit

it, but there is a lot of truth in Hal's words. The best part was that I didn't even have to ask him.

"Speaking of asking," Shirley went on, "I never asked if you minded if I pretend you're my father. I hope not, because now I'm going to pretend for real.

"There are a lot of things I need to get straight, and I think you can help me figure them out—like why Anna never told me you died, and why Grandma didn't either. How long did they think they could keep me in the dark? After six years, I now know you are dead. There is a body and nothing else. Or is there something else?

"Grandma says there is a reason for everything. I think I know why I reached for you when I saw you lying on the ground. It was like reaching for my father, who I miss so much. He wasn't there, but you were.

"So I guess the reason I am asking you to be a substitute for my dad for a while is that I have a lot of unfinished father matters to finish, and you won't tell me to be quiet or switch the conversation to ballet or to the next guest star on *The Ed Sullivan Show.*

"One thing is that I have never asked Anna why she felt the need to scissor you out of that photograph. If she intends for me to forget you, I will not.

"And why did Aunt Rosalie say your heart was broken? Did someone break it? Or did it break from being old and worn out like that plate that gets more cracked every time Hal drops his fork on it? I will get to the bottom of that by hook or by crook, as Grandma says.

"You have shown me that life doesn't last forever. So I am going to make a list of things I need to do, not necessarily in the order that I will do them, because some things require a ton of courage, even for Pippi Longstocking, and might have to be moved to the bottom for another time.

"Here goes:

"First, I *will* tell Mr. Merrill tomorrow at school that he made a mistake by accusing me of something I didn't do. (I'm putting this at the top of the list, despite the fact that it will require a ton of courage, since it is already almost tomorrow.)

"Second, I *will* go to Lake Winnipesaukee and not to Breezy Bay Day Camp this summer.

"Third, I *will* help Mr. Bickerstaff change his attitude toward Mustard, or I will adopt him (Mustard—not Mr. Bickerstaff).

"Fourth, I *will* tell Anna that I hate being sent to the bathroom on Saturday mornings, taking ballet lessons, following the Safe-at-Home Doctrine, and pretending to like her friend Hal and calling him Big Daddy. (I will not be mendacious anymore and say that I like things when I don't.)

"Fifth, I *will* play spin the bottle and make sure Maury Gordon plays at the same time.

"Sixth, I *will* continue to save for an attached house till I get one."

"Who are you talking to, Shirley?" Phillie asked, materializing out of nowhere, holding on to his bike and a flashlight. This time, Mustard did bark. "Grandma says that people who talk to themselves have money in the bank."

"Well, I do have money in the bank," Shirley answered, jumping up. "For your information, Hal just gave me my allowance for this week. So Grandma is right as usual."

"You don't usually talk to yourself," said Phillie, sticking to the subject. He parked his bike. Then he and his black Converse sneakers and flashlight came closer. "I promise I won't think you're crazy if you tell me. No secrets, remember?"

Shirley still wasn't sure if she wanted to tell Phillie about Mouse, so she said, "What are you doing here anyway, Phillie?"

"Father's Day was done at my house, so I came over to beat you in poker or Monopoly or Scrabble. Or all three."

"That'll be the day," said Shirley.

"I'm waiting," said Phillie.

With her mind now made up, Shirley said, "If you

really want to know, I was talking to my father—who is being represented by a dead mouse." Shirley stared Phillie straight in the eye to gauge his reaction. "If you say one bad thing, Phillip Barrett—even *yuck*—you better go home," she warned. Then she showed him the checkbook box. "This is Mouse."

Phillie kneeled down on the warm, dark soil and clicked on his flashlight to get a good look. Without waiting for Shirley to explain further, he said, "I understand the whole, entire thing, Shirl. It's what you have to do to fix yourself now that you've found out the truth about your dad. Like you always try to fix everything that's broken. But the truth is that Mouse is going to start to smell soon," he added, "like the meat in Mr. Emmett's butcher shop did last year when it was really hot and all he had going was one single standing fan rotating on the saw-dust floor."

"I do *not* want to bury him," Shirley said with conviction, "if that's what you're suggesting."

"Okay," said Phillie, "then we need to think of something else." Phillie looked up at Shirley. He pointed to two large ants crawling around Mouse's left eye. "Those ants have lots of cousins," he said, "who are all invited to the picnic. And this is only the beginning. In the summer a corpse turns into a skeleton really fast. I guess we can say this mouse is a corpse, too, since we don't have your real father here." Phillie stood up and started pacing, then said, "I am almost positive that I have a solution to the problem. I watched a whole program once on Channel 13 about exactly this. Ready to hear about it?"

"Of course I am," said Shirley.

Phillie, suddenly full of mischief, said, "I need to ask you something first."

"What?"

"Why are baseball players so cool?"

"Why?" Shirley asked, eager to get to the heart of the matter.

"Because they have a lot of fans!" said Phillie.

"Phillie!" said Shirley. "Cut the baloney."

"Okay," said Phillie. "I'll cut it. There's this famous mummy called the Ice Man whose over 5,300-year-old body was discovered frozen solid. Everything about him was still perfect: his blood, his muscles, his teeth, his skull, his bones, his hair, and—can you believe it—even his heart. Everything! So my guess is that you'll be able to keep your mummy mouse perfectly preserved also, until you are ready not to. And where will we do this, Phillie, you ask, since we do *not* live in the frozen tundra or at the Arctic Circle?"

But Shirley didn't need to ask. She had been hanging

on every word and could now conclusively say with Phillie: "In the freezer!"

• • • • •

While Phillie watched a dog and monkey ride a pony on *The Ed Sullivan Show* with Grandma on the couch, and Anna talked on the phone to Aunt Claire, extending the cord to its fullest length so she could sit on a dinette chair, Shirley slipped into the kitchen to put the checkbook box in the freezer with the body of Mouse inside. She slid the box under a bag of Birds Eye frozen spinach.

Shirley washed her hands like she'd seen Anna and Grandma do when they came back from the cemetery after Maury Gordon's grandpa died last year—to keep death out of their apartment. *Little do they know,* thought Shirley, *but death is definitely in our apartment. By invitation.*

After Phillie left to finish his Sam Houston biography that was due tomorrow at school, Shirley took his place on the couch. Grandma put down her knitting needles and patted the space under her arm so Shirley could burrow with her nose and rest her tired head on Grandma's big pillow chest. *The Ed Sullivan Show* was over for this Sunday.

"You're cuckoo to love an old voman like me," said Grandma out of the blue.

Shirley wanted to be part of Grandma forever. She gently pressed the rubbery veins on Grandma's hand until they sprang back up. Then she turned Grandpa's wedding ring, which swam on Grandma's finger, until the three colored stones were on top: red, blue, green. Shirley thought, *If God were a woman, she'd be Grandma. There is nothing to fix. She is as perfect as a star.*

Shirley looked up. "I wish I had pink cheeks like yours, Grandma," she said.

"Only peasants have pink cheeks," Grandma answered. "I vish I had pale cheeks like yours."

Shirley thought of Mouse in the freezer and was inexplicably happy. And, of course, she had Grandma.

Then the very thought of no Grandma made Shirley immensely sad. She framed Grandma's face with both of her hands, touched her red-orange earrings, round like tiny tomatoes, and the soft lobes of Grandma's ears. Then through burning tears Shirley said, "Why don't both of us go to Lake Winnipesaukee this summer and let Anna observe the Safe-at-Home Doctrine by herself?"

Grandma didn't answer. She must have thought Shirley was joking.

Shirley turned off the TV. She helped Grandma put her hair into night braids and then make the couch into her bed by removing the giant cushions and spreading a sheet with ballerinas on the flat part. Shirley went to the closet and got Grandma's pillow and the patched summer blanket made from squares of old sheets. Then while Grandma went into the bathroom without her teeth (she had put them in a glass with water on the coffee table), Shirley stood at the living room window in the dark, watching the white lights of airplanes as they made their turns to LaGuardia Airport. She thought of going to school tomorrow and of the first and perhaps most difficult of her "I *will*" promises. "I hope I can do it," she whispered.

Chapter 12
THE EGG THAT BROKE
THE CHICKEN'S BACK

THE NOISY WHIRRING OF THE ELECTRIC SILEX JUICER WAS Shirley's alarm clock. Every school morning before Anna left for work, she cut in half, then squeezed, four plump oranges over the white spinning top of the small machine for Shirley. The fresh juice went down the porcelain spout (the pits were caught in a strainer) and then into the wide-mouthed antique glass from Mr. Joseph's that was exclusively Shirley's for orange juice. An almond tart in a little aluminum cup waited next to the glass. Anna placed a small saucer over the glass so that no flies or dust would fall in. She started what would be two soft-boiled eggs as soon as she saw Shirley coming out of the bedroom all brushed and dressed for school.

It was a fate worse than death for Shirley to eat those

eggs, and a puzzle to her that Anna, after so many tries, had not learned how to make them edible. Eggshells and lumps of salt sat in the gelatinous lukewarm mess.

Today was no different.

"Open your mouth!" demanded Anna, sounding like a general in the army. "If I didn't love you, I wouldn't care what you ate."

"Mnnn!" said Shirley, attempting to say *No!* without using her lips for clarity because that would mean she'd have to open her mouth.

"Open up," said Anna, "or you'll miss the bus." In spite of the fact that Shirley had at least thirty minutes till the school bus came and it was Anna who would have to walk extra-fast to the subway to get to Mr. Joseph's in Manhattan if she hovered any longer over Shirley and the inedible eggs.

Enraged, Anna tugged twice on Shirley's braid with her free hand like she was ringing a bell. Shirley's mouth opened, not in submission, but in surprise. Whereupon Anna, sensing victory, threw a spoonful of the disgusting yellow jellyfish-like glop down Shirley's throat.

"You'll thank me for your strong bones when you're older, Shirley," said Anna.

Shirley gagged. "No I won't," she said, wiping her mouth and taking a bite of the almond cake to diffuse the putrid taste of the eggs. Then Shirley said, "Okay, that's enough. No more."

But Anna insisted on finishing the job.

"Mnnn-mnnn," said Shirley through closed lips.

So Anna pulled again. Only this time, Grandma was there to pull, too.

"Are you crazy, Anna?" asked Grandma in Russian, grabbing her by the waist. Then in English she said, "Leave the child alone."

Which Anna did, slamming the Pyrex custard cup down on the table. The cup bounced and the spoon went flying. Then so did Anna. Out the door and over the bridge.

While Grandma went to the bathroom to undo her night braids, Shirley visited the freezer. She was happy to see that Phillie's prediction that Mouse would be perfectly preserved in every way was true. And now, just like her father, Mouse would be there whenever she needed him.

"I'm not a child," she told Mouse. "I'm almost twelve. What doesn't Anna understand? You used to let me try things on my own. Like riding my bike without training wheels. When I fell, you knew it would make me better at it the next time. I see that now. It's like sinking or swimming. How do I make everyone else see it?"

Shirley thought she heard her father say, "Tell them the truth, Shirley girl, even if it hurts."

. . . . .

Most mornings when it wasn't raining, Shirley and Maury liked to play off-the-wall before the school bus came. At the back entrance to Sparrowood Gardens, against one of two brick walls of apartments that faced the driveway, Shirley threw her ball and cleanly jumped over it before it could hit the ground and bounce off the other wall. When it was Maury's turn, he threw Shirley's ball against the highest part of one wall, hoping the ball would ricochet off the other wall so that either he or Shirley could catch it. As luck would have it, though, the ball slipped out of Maury's hand and landed on the roof.

"Oh crap," Maury said, pulling on his tie with both hands. "Sorry, Shirley," he said. "I'll get it down for you as soon as we get home. Don't worry, my ball is at school in my desk for recess."

But Shirley did worry. She would not consider going an entire day without the blue ball in her pocket.

As if her life depended on it, Shirley flung open the door to the apartment building and rushed up the rungs of the stationary iron ladder in the hallway. It was tricky business climbing the ladder in a dress. Not to mention dangerous. The bottom of her dress got caught under her feet with every step. Luke would definitely have told Shirley that he would be happy to climb up there and get her ball.

When Shirley got to the top of the ladder, she lifted the metal cover on the ceiling with her head and ran out onto the flat roof to retrieve the precious ball, which was trapped in the rain gutter at the very edge.

"Wow!" Maury said when Shirley pushed open the door from the inside a short time later.

Shirley shoved the ball back into her pocket. "Faster than the speed of light," she said, sweat trickling down from her head to her neck to her back.

Maury smiled as he picked up Shirley's books, bound together with a thick rubber strap, and walked the few feet to the bus stop.

Shirley and Maury joined the line of Sparrowood Gardens kids waiting for the bus: Curtis Karl bearing a purple scar on his chin from falling on a pencil point last year, Beryl Abbie singing her favorite song, Dale Rosenberger bending her middle finger all the way back to show that she was double-jointed, Laurence-with-a-*u* Livingstone babbling about how there would be hardly any work to do during the last days before school ended.

"Yeah," agreed Maury and Shirley at the same time.

As she waited, Shirley checked out the cars on the road, each one going someplace important to the driver. She liked cars like Phillie did. A VW bug happened to stop opposite the bus stop, taking its place in the long line of traffic headed down the hill to the light. No one took much notice of the pale green Volkswagen at first, except for Shirley. She thought the small car was nice, until she saw who was driving it. Mr. Merrill looked over at the kids assembled at the bus stop. He waved. Shirley waved back, automatically, like when someone asked how you were, and you said, "Fine." She clutched the ball in her pocket. Her knees felt flimsy, like paper.

"Hey! There's Mr. Merrill!" said Maury. Looking across the street, the other kids waved as the VW started down the hill when the light changed.

• • • • •

That morning, Mr. Merrill returned the spelling tests from Friday. Shirley was quietly proud when she saw that her perfect record would remain intact.

"Nice work," whispered Barry-the-Brain.

Then Mr. Merrill gave the class a surprise free-writing period. "You can write about anything on your minds," he said. "What you will remember about sixth grade, what you will do this summer, what you want to be someday. Anything. I will read your essays and give them back to you. Let yourselves go. Spelling doesn't count."

I know what I'm going to write, Shirley thought. *How perfect.*

Dear Mr. Merrill,

I am not a plagiarist and I will never be one. I have my own opinions and a few different styles of writing that change depending on what I want the words to say. That's what writers do. You have always told us to trust our first instincts because they are usually correct. In this case, however, your first instinct was wrong. My essay deserved to be sent to WNYC Radio with the others. My father told me to tell the truth, which I am doing now.

With all due respect,
Shirley Alice Burns

Glancing up, Shirley noticed that Mr. Merrill had begun patrolling the aisles to check on each student's progress. Before he could get to her desk, she folded the letter in half, then in quarters, then in eighths, and put it in her pocket next to her ball, thinking how hard it was to let it go. To let it be read. *But I'll figure it out,* her lips silently said.

By the time Mr. Merrill reached her desk, Shirley had a new piece of paper in front of her and was writing about Mickey Mantle, the best hitter on the Yankees. Shirley smiled as she wrote. "Mickey Mantle wears the number 7. Maybe it's his lucky number."

Mr. Merrill went on to the next desk.

After lunch, Barry-the-Brain offered his unopened bag of Fritos to Shirley at their shared double desk.

"Thanks," she said.

Then Barry said, "Would you go with me to the sixth-grade prom, Shirley? I really like you."

Shirley was so taken aback that she couldn't think of anything to say. She finally managed, "I didn't even know there was a sixth-grade prom." It was the truth.

Barry, sensing the awkward moment, said, "I mimeographed the announcements for Mr. Merrill before school. He'll probably hand them out to us today before we go home."

Then Barry showed Shirley the photograph that was in his desk.

"Look, it's you!" he said. The photo was from a fifth-grade bulletin-board display that had pictured each student holding up a book that he or she was reading. Shirley had tossed her photo in the trash, but Barry had obviously fished it out and kept it.

Shirley smiled.

. . . . .

That afternoon, Mr. Merrill gave the class the announcements, saying, "There'll be great music at the prom, delicious refreshments, and all kinds of decorations—a party in the gym for the entire sixth grade right after lunch. The school bus will be waiting for those of you who usually take it to go home. Everyone will have a dandy time."

Shirley could see some kids wriggling in their seats— like Marcy Bronson, maybe because she was afraid no one would ask her to dance, and Robin Miller, because excitement of any sort usually made her throw up. Next to Shirley, Barry twirled a pencil. His fingers made the eraser, the yellow body, and the point go round and round like a rotisserie chicken on a spit.

"What do we wear, Mr. Merrill?" Beth Ann Lanier asked. Shirley knew Beth Ann liked Mitchell Payne, a boy in another class.

"Something nice, stupid," said Lannie Kaufman.

Shirley turned to Barry. "Thanks for asking me, Barry. I'll let you know very soon."

· · · · ·

On the bus ride home, Maury said to Shirley, "Will you go with me to the prom?" Almost immediately Shirley's stomach started making gurgling noises like a slow drain after a bubble bath—*glub glub glub*—at the thought of telling Barry why she couldn't go with him. But how indescribably excited she was at the thought of going to the prom with Maury!

· · · · ·

"Sometimes life is pretty hard, but sometimes it's okay," Shirley told Mouse that night. "Two boys in my class asked me to go to the prom. Saying no to Barry will not be my favorite thing. He is dandruffy and bad with a baseball bat, but very generous with Fritos and definitely the smartest kid in our class by far. I wrote Mr. Merrill a letter about how I feel about being called a plagiarist, but I didn't give it to him yet. I'm still scared. Petrified, if you really want to know." Then, "Good night, Mouse. I'm so glad you're here."

In the bedroom, the window handle came off in

Shirley's hand when she turned it to let in some cool night air. She got her screwdriver from the bathroom and in a few minutes had secured the handle so it worked again. Crickets, doves, and Luke sang their separate-but-together night songs. Shirley remembered Pippi Longstocking's declaration "Isn't it glorious to be alive!" and she felt peaceful.

Next she said her prayers: "God bless Anna, Mouse, Grandma, Aunt Rosalie, Uncle Rod, Laurel, Ruthie, Steve, Phillie, and Scott. And Aunt Claire, Uncle Bill, Esther, and Arlene. And Natalie and Mustard. And please do not let me get sent to the principal's office when I give my letter to Mr. Merrill. I also hope his feelings won't be hurt. Because he is a good teacher 'after all is said and done.'" Shirley actually laughed. *I'm loony,* she thought. But she'd heard those words on the radio so many times in a commercial for Palisades Amusement Park that she had them memorized. A lot of kids in her class had gone with their families to New Jersey, where the amusement park was. *New Jersey is another place I haven't been,* thought Shirley.

Shirley heard Anna and Grandma in the living room having one of their heated discussions. She reached down under her bed and found the book called *The Stork Didn't Bring You,* which Aunt Rosalie had ceremoniously bestowed upon her recently because Anna was uncomfortable talking about the facts of life—or else she had no clue about them—like genetics, for example.

"Your father wasn't around long enough for you to get his genes, Shirley," Anna once said in a huff of nonsense.

Shirley read by the light of her bedside lamp, no need for a flashlight under the covers, as Anna, apparently very involved with Grandma, had forgotten that the hour had passed to come in and say good night.

Growing up isn't easy, the facts-of-life book said.

"You said it!" Shirley agreed. She absorbed everything about girls' and boys' differences until her eyes stung. Even about how her father played a big role in her existence despite what Anna had told her.

And *social security*: it had a different meaning in the book than the meaning Shirley knew. She read:

Social security (not the kind deducted from dad's income)—*or Anna's paycheck*, Shirley thought—is an essential requisite to every human life. That inside-yourself feeling that you "belong" where you are; that you're wanted because you're YOU; that the things you do for others are appreciated because YOU did them—that's social security.

Then Shirley heard the living room go quiet. Anna and Grandma had concluded their argument and Anna was now belting out the song "Oh, My Papa" in the shower like Eddie Fisher. The words, loud and clear, made Shirley want to rush in there to tell her to stop.

How come Anna gets to miss her father and I don't? Shirley thought.

Anna, who claimed she was Grandpa's favorite daughter, had told Shirley stories about how he used to dance on the table when he was happy, make wine in their bathtub, and give out candy to the kids, extra to Anna, every Friday when he came home from work.

But I know almost nothing about my father. I don't even remember what color eyes he had.

Shirley threw *The Stork* across the room and turned off the light just as Anna came in to get her own book and to say, "Good night. Iloveyou."

Chapter 13
OPENING UP

ON TUESDAY MORNING WHEN SHE HEARD THE WHIRRING OF THE
juice machine, Shirley decided she did not want to go to
school.

"My throat hurts," she told Anna, putting her hands
in front of her neck. "And I'm tired, and I have a dry
cough and a drippy nose. Sore throats are going around,
but there is nothing to worry about. I'll be fine by tomorrow." (Shirley would never miss a Wednesday at school
because that was the day Mrs. Greif brought French to
Class 6-1.)

Anna felt Shirley's forehead with her lips. "No fever,"
she told her, adding an "Iloveyou" for good measure. Then
Anna was out the door, looking like a model in *Vogue*.

No school meant there would be no soft-boiled eggs.
Shirley snickered.

"Why didn't I think of that before?" she asked Mouse in the freezer.

Shirley saw Grandma, scissors pointed down, heading outside to the stoop for a haircut. Shirley closed the freezer door.

"Don't you need a mirror?" Shirley asked.

"No. I just hold vone handful like this, and another handful like this, and the middle part like this and cut straight across and I'm done!" said Grandma, demonstrating. "That vay, no little pieces of hair fall on Anna's clean floor. And there is less vork for Grandma!"

Shirley went back to the freezer. She told Mouse, "You make me feel lucky and rich and strong. Thank you for listening."

When Shirley heard Grandma's shoes padding back toward the kitchen, she whispered, "Talk to you later, Mouse."

"Are you hungry, Shirley?" Grandma asked over the hum of the refrigerator, her hair short, even, and stick-straight like uncooked spaghetti.

"I was," said Shirley, not knowing if Grandma was aware of the open freezer or not. "I thought I'd have a little ice cream." Shirley found a spoon, opened the freezer again, and stuck the spoon into some cherry vanilla.

"Vhy don't vee bake, Shirley, my sunny child?" asked Grandma.

Grandma and Shirley made a batch of Pillsbury buttermilk biscuits. Grandma didn't mind when Shirley peeled the warm American cheese off the tops of three of them because she herself preferred the doughy middles. *Even if Grandma preferred the warm cheese part like I do, she still wouldn't mind,* thought Shirley.

"Whoever invented tea in a bag was vone smart cookie," said Grandma at the table. "Maybe it vas Mr. Lipton." Grandma dripped amber drops of honey and dunked the soft part of a buttermilk biscuit in Mr. Lipton's clever invention.

Then she sang a song she'd heard Bing Crosby sing on the radio. "Did you ever see a dream valking? Vell, I did. Did you ever hear a dream talking? Vell, I did."

And Shirley melted, like the cheese on top of the biscuits.

"Let's fit your sundress and your new shorts," said Grandma. "You can pick out the buttons from the big jar." Grandma was proud of the fact that she never used a paper pattern to cut out her designs. She did everything by instinct.

Grandma sat with her short legs stretched out on the floor as stiff as her yardstick. The fan of straight pins in her mouth reminded Shirley of a porcupine. A soft, round porcupine in a yellow, red, pink, blue, and green dress with a painted rooster pin fastened to the center of the

Belgian lace collar. When Grandma had pins in her mouth she had no choice but to hum, so this time Shirley sang the words to the "dream walking" song.

When the pins holding up the hems of the shorts scratched Shirley's thighs, she didn't say *Ouch! Chort!* (Russian for "Damn!") or *Zut!* (French for "Damn!"—say: "Suit!" but with a *z*).

Who am I to grouse when Grandma's doing all the work on a very boiling day, Shirley thought.

"Thanks, Grandma," she said, overflowing with love.

Grandma spit the pins into her hand. "You're very velcome," she said. "Now please vould you stand still."

"I'm going to wear my new sundress and my new shorts when I go to Lake Winnipesaukee," said Shirley. "When *we* go to Lake Winnipesaukee. I never saw *you* wear shorts, Grandma."

"I vear shorts," she answered. "They're under my dress. Look." Grandma lifted up her dress to reveal a pair of long hot-pink underpants made of heavy cotton jersey.

That was Grandma. She liked what she liked. And no one could change her mind.

"Turn," she said, tapping Shirley's leg with four fingers.

"So will you wear the blue-and-black bathing suit with the accordion skirt to Lake Winnipesaukee? Anna doesn't know it yet, but I'm going to get a new bathing suit. By the way, I am *not* going to Breezy Bay Day Camp this summer. Or ever again."

Grandma stopped measuring. She stopped pinning. She spilled herself over onto her right side like a sack of flour. She propelled herself up. "Good for you, Shirley," she said. "It's time for you to stick up for yourself." Then Grandma said, "I have something to tell you."

"What?" Shirley asked.

"I vould like to go to Vinnipesaukee, too. But I vill be busy setting up my new apartment. I'm moving, my sunny child. I found a place, as big as a shoebox, but it vill be all mine. Vhat do you think of your grandma now, Shirley?" Grandma's false teeth beamed pearly white as she smiled wide.

"You're moving?" asked Shirley, her heart pounding so fast in her chest that she thought it might come bursting out. "Why do you want to do that?

"It's time," said Grandma. "You're a big girl. You don't need me to vatch vhat you're doing every second like I used to. My lease starts on July first. I'll be two blocks away. That's far enough and close enough, too."

Shirley suddenly wanted to be alone. Even away from Grandma. She rushed to her room and slammed the door. Tears stood in her eyes. "Why doesn't anyone ever ask my opinion? *Damn, chort, zut,*" she said aloud. *What next?* she wondered.

"Shirley, my sunny child, vhat's the matter?" Grandma asked, knocking and then opening the door. "I'm only moving down the street. Come out and let's have some lunch."

After Shirley finished a bowl of cold cucumber soup, some pumpernickel bread, and a frosty glass of apricot nectar that Grandma had just bought yesterday with a coupon at Smilen Brothers, she felt better.

Then she told Grandma just about everything that was unfair in her life, crying so hard that Grandma said, "I can hardly understand vhat you are saying when you are crying like that."

So Shirley stopped crying and hiccupped instead.

"I'm so sorry, Shirley, my sunny child," Grandma said over and over.

Finally, Shirley stopped hiccupping and tried again, more slowly. "It's so hard having a mother un-invite you when someone invites you year after year on your dream trip because she wants to keep you away from everything risky. So she can monitor every move you make, like you're a remote-control child, ordering you to stay in the bathroom, take ballet, go to baby day camp, eat soft-boiled eggs, and write a Father's Day card to someone who makes you jump a mile when he drops his fork onto his plate on purpose if you don't pay attention to his dumb shoe stories. Which leads me to what I have been wanting to ask you, Grandma."

"Vhat is it?" Grandma asked.

"Why couldn't I know when my father died? When you knew?"

Strangely, Shirley perceived, Grandma did not look surprised.

"I vill tell you, Shirley," Grandma said. And then she looked as if she might change her mind and not tell. But Grandma did not change her mind that afternoon.

She took off her glasses and cleaned them, sighing a moist cloud onto each lens. She turned the ring with the colored stones till the stones were on top. And slurped a mouthful of tea. She checked her watch and reached for one of her tiny tomato earrings.

"I think you vill understand that I couldn't tell you before because Anna did not vant you to know. She thought you vere very little for such big news. The truth is that I needed a place to live because I vas afraid to live alone vhen Grandpa died. Then vhen Anna said I could live vith her and vith you—to help vhen she had to go to vork after she told your father she didn't vant to be together vith him anymore—I had to live by her rules. So I vas not free to tell you. But I vas so happy that I said okay. To everything."

"You were afraid to live alone before? But now you're not?" Shirley asked.

"That's right," said Grandma.

"How come?" asked Shirley, caught off guard by Grandma's revelation.

"I think I understand the vorld better," said Grandma. "And I'm too old for Anna's rules."

"So am I," said Shirley.

And Grandma smiled.

"Does Anna know you're moving?" asked Shirley.

"I think everyone in Sparrovood Gardens knows I'm moving. I told Augusta," said Grandma. "It's vhat Anna and I talked about last night."

"I'm proud of you, Grandma," said Shirley.

"Me too," said Grandma.

Chapter 14
IN ABSENTIA

THAT AFTERNOON, BERYL ABBIE RAN ALL THE WAY FROM THE BUS
stop, the red ribbon attached to her skinny pigtail threat-
ening to become unattached, to tell Shirley her big news.

"Guess what, Shirley Burns?" Beryl Abbie asked, out
of breath.

"What?" asked Shirley, sitting outside on the stoop in
front of their apartment, reading and re-reading her letter to Mr. Merrill that she had, in fact, decided to put in
his school mailbox tomorrow. Shirley was sure she knew
what Beryl Abbie couldn't wait to share, but she would
not spoil the younger girl's surprise for all the one-dollar
bills in Hal's crummy pocket.

"I sat next to Maury Gordon two times today on the
bus!" Beryl Abbie shouted.

"Lucky duck!" said Shirley. "How was it?"

"We sang the whole way to school. And then we sang again coming home," Beryl Abbie said. "Will you be absent again tomorrow?"

"Nope," said Shirley. "I'm not sick anymore. And I have some important business to take care of. And French with Mrs. Greif. Sorry."

"Maybe we can sit three in a seat," said Beryl Abbie.

"Maybe," said Shirley. Then she mumbled inaudibly, "When the moon turns green," quoting what Anna said whenever Shirley asked to go to a party at Sharon Levitt's house.

Shirley went inside. She sat down at Anna's desk and rewrote her letter—in pen this time. When she was finished, she folded it in three the long way, found a legal-size envelope in a drawer, printed *Mr. Merrill* and *Official Business* on the outside, and slipped the letter in. Shirley was about to lick the envelope when she remembered what Anna always said—"You get cancer from doing that"—so she wet her finger under the faucet instead.

She put the envelope in her notebook to take to school tomorrow and went back outside, where she started to bounce her ball and watch for Anna to come walking up the street from the bus stop, home from work.

When at last Shirley saw Anna, she stopped bouncing and ran to greet her. Anna's smile was as bright as the sun when she saw Shirley. Everything else between them

135

was forgotten, as it always was when they were back to-gether again.

"Hi, doll!" said Anna so loud that Shirley was posi-tive the people in the next development—Arrowbrook Gardens, where Grandma was moving—could hear her. "How are you feeling?" Anna asked.

"Much better," said Shirley, cringing only slightly. She went to the other side of Anna to share the carrying of a huge square package that Anna said was a surprise.

"Wait till you see what I bought!"

The package said *Buy Wise* on the wrapping, so Shir-ley knew it was not another unnecessary purchase from Mr. Joseph's. It was heavy and awkward to carry.

"You could be an actress like Audrey Hepburn," said Shirley, looking up proudly at Anna, then down at her meticulously polished red toes sticking out of the fronts of Hal's gifted shoes, matching her lipstick. Anna's *Le langage des fleurs* ("the language of the flowers") dress, Shirley's favorite, was perfectly pressed even after a long day. Anna was one of those mothers, Shirley knew, who would not be happy staying at home like Dale Rosenberg-er's mother or Monica Callahan's or Beryl Abbie's.

When they got inside, Shirley asked, "Can I open it now?" as Grandma and Anna gathered around to watch as if a blue-ribbon ceremony were about to take place in their living room.

Phillie let the screen door bang as he joined the party. "What's in the package?" he asked.

"We're about to find out," said Shirley.

"Wait till you see," said Anna, looking at Phillie over her shoulder.

"Wow!" said Shirley as she pulled off the brown paper.

It was a brand-new white metal fan!

"Let's try it out!" said Anna, plugging it in.

Shirley stood next to Phillie, who stood next to Grandma, who stood next to Anna, and felt the deliciously cool wind on her face.

"We can move it from room to room all summer, you know," said Anna. "Sleeping will be so much nicer."

"You should get one for your apartment," Shirley told Grandma.

"I vill," said Grandma.

"I came over to tell you that Grandma is moving," Phillie whispered to Shirley. "But I see you already know."

Phillie watched Shirley eat a quick dinner of Grandma's hard-as-a-hockey-puck hamburger with a scallion, cucumber, and tomato salad. The hamburger had been made earlier in the day so the kitchen would have a chance to cool off before nighttime. Shirley set aside a small piece of meat for Natalie.

"Are you hungry, Phillie?" Grandma asked, although

she knew the kids in Phillie's family always ate by themselves at five so Aunt Rosalie could have a romantic dinner with Uncle Rod when he came home from work.

"Nah," said Phillie. "We had disgusting liver."

Shirley imagined herself at the dinner table with the Barrett kids, elbowing Phillie next to her because it was so hot, wiping her mouth with only half a napkin to save money, eating the last French fry for spite so none of the other kids would get it. Giving most of her liver to Porky, who ate anything—even liver—when Aunt Rosalie wasn't looking. Wearing a polo shirt that said LAUREL-RUTHIESTEVESHIRLEYPHILLIESCOTT.

"How about that fan!" said Anna, taking off her high heels and then spreading her long arms like wings in front of the slowly rotating starlike blade, her fingers as graceful and relaxed as if she were executing a pose at the Bolshoi Ballet.

"Good invention," said Grandma.

"I'm ready to pick out my Aurora Road Race set," Phillie told Shirley as she gulped her milk.

• • • • •

Phillie and Shirley rode their bikes to the Barretts' house. Then they walked the eight blocks to the department store, which was open late on Tuesdays.

"I make three dollars an hour now at Red's," said Phillie proudly. "I got a raise." Phillie flashed his stash of cash, which he usually kept hidden from his brothers and sisters in an old Atlantic City saltwater taffy bank made of cardboard.

Shirley couldn't believe how much money a kid could make.

When they got to the toy department, Phillie said, "I have enough money for two fancier cars than the ones that come with the set. One for me and one for you, Shirl."

"Thanks!" said Shirley, dazzled by all the choices.

After studying each car through the plastic window of the package, Shirley opted for the sleek, sporty silver Corvette.

"Did you ever see anything more beautiful than this?" asked Phillie, showing Shirley his selection: the Batmobile, the most expensive car Aurora made, at five dollars. Phillie hugged it to his chest.

Shirley read the Road Race box while they waited on the checkout line:

```
Down goes the green flag and they're off—
zooming along the straightaway at 150
scale mph! The ultimate in table-top
racing: gives you twice the action in half
```

the space. Lets you re-create any race
course in the world.

Phillie always knew what he wanted and worked hard to get it. Although he had never seen Hal's *YCDBSOYA* tie clip, Shirley knew he would really like it. The old admiration for her favorite cousin filled her up till she thought she'd burst like the aluminum-foil Jiffy Pop container Aunt Rosalie once left for too long on the gas burner till the popcorn exploded all over the kitchen. Phillie never let grass grow under his feet, an expression Shirley had first heard when Anna tried to convince Grandma that Hal would make a good husband and father because he was not lazy.

"Vhy don't you look through *my* glasses," Shirley remembered Grandma telling Anna. And they argued till the cows came home. Another of Anna's favorite phrases.

When they got to Phillie's house, he and Shirley went down to the basement where Uncle Rod was sitting in his recliner. Uncle Rod and Phillie each had their own private enclaves down there away from the noise and chaos of upstairs.

"Whatcha got?" Uncle Rod asked. Then he added, "Hi, Shirley, the best ballplayer I know next to Mickey Mantle!"

Shirley stayed for a while to help Phillie set up the Road Race tracks on the long wooden table. When Shirley had to leave, she was happy knowing that Uncle Rod would finish the job with Phillie. It was getting dark, and tomorrow was a school day.

"See ya, Shirl," said Phillie. "Thanks for coming with me."

"See ya," said Shirley. She gave Uncle Rod a big hug. "Wait till my cool Corvette leaves every one of your cars in the dust!" she told Phillie.

• • • • •

Grandma was outside on the bench with the Pigeon People when Shirley rode by on her bike. She heard Grandma say, "Sam used to buy me the biggest box of licorice from Blum's in San Francisco. It had purple flowers on the outside."

"Isaac used to buy me Barricini's," bragged Augusta. "And I didn't even like chocolate."

Shirley stopped to pet Mustard, who was sitting on his side of the stoop with Mr. Bickerstaff.

"He likes you," Mr. Bickerstaff told Shirley, offering her a Chiclet.

"He likes you, too," Shirley admitted, shaking a Chiclet out of the small yellow box. She bumped her bike up the steps and into their apartment, where Anna was watching *Perry Mason*, a show about lawyers, on TV.

"I can't smoke because the fan blows the ashes from the ashtray all over the place," Anna said. "And I just broke my back dusting."

"Good," said Shirley.

· · · · ·

When Shirley got into bed that night, she noticed her bookmark was not where she'd left it in *Cheaper by the Dozen*. It took her a while to find the lost place by reading backward from where the bookmark had been randomly dropped in. *Anna must have moved my library books when she was cleaning and the bookmark slipped out,* Shirley thought, surprised at how unnerved she felt when she didn't know what was going on in the story. You can't just keep reading if you don't know what came before.

Then, not being able to concentrate, Shirley put down *Cheaper by the Dozen* and headed to the kitchen. Grandma was on the couch reading *War and Peace*, the Russian version of course. And Anna, Shirley noticed, was now in the bathroom. Shirley smelled cigarette smoke.

It was a perfectly clear night to watch the low-flying

airplanes turning toward LaGuardia. Red lights blinked a warning to other planes. Intense white lights remained steady like two huge eyes in the sky.

"I'm going places, too," Shirley said to Mouse before heading back to her room.

Chapter 15
TAKING CARE OF BUSINESS

WHEN THEY GOT TO SCHOOL THE NEXT DAY, SHIRLEY TOLD MAURY she had some private business to take care of in the office. "If you want, you can wait for me in the hall."

So that's what Maury did while Shirley deposited the *Official Business* envelope in Mr. Merrill's mail slot. Shirley had penciled in an infinitesimally small number 6 on the lower left corner of the envelope for luck. She didn't know what time teachers usually got their mail, but she expected that she'd know when Mr. Merrill got his. *Either he'll be ripping mad,* Shirley thought, *or he'll be contrite.* That was one of the meaty words she'd saved; it meant he'd be sorry he'd accused her of plagiarism.

"What do you think, Mouse?" Shirley whispered. "Will this be the day Mr. Merrill realizes he made a big mistake?" Shirley had realized that she no longer needed to actually look at Mouse or even be at home when she talked to him.

The second thing Shirley did that morning was remember her promise to let Barry-the-Brain know what she was going to do about the prom.

"I have something for you," said Barry.

"I've decided about the prom," said Shirley before Barry could pull out the snack-size bag of Fritos from his desk. Which seemed weird to her because it wasn't after lunch yet.

"Are you going with me?" Barry asked, smiling brightly, dislodging a few dandruff flakes as he adjusted his glasses.

Shirley had been thinking about her answer. "Maury Gordon also asked me to go to the prom with him. I like you both, so maybe the three of us could go to the prom together. Would you mind?"

"Great!" Barry answered. "This is what I wanted to give you." He reached all the way in toward the back of his desk, not for the familiar bag of Fritos as expected, but for something else.

"Girls don't usually have one," he told her, "but you're a girl who should."

It was his Louisville Slugger baseball glove. Shirley nearly fainted.

She felt the leather and smelled it and slipped her left

hand inside, each finger finding its place in the glove, which was like new. Incredible. At first Shirley thought she should give the glove back. That's what Anna would tell her to do. Then she thought she shouldn't. Barry-the-Brain looked so happy. And what would he do with a baseball glove anyway.

"Thanks a million billion!" she said.

Shirley couldn't believe how nice Barry was. How glad she was that he had accepted her reply to his prom invitation.

Mr. Merrill addressed the class. "You all seem very chatty today. It must be because it's the first day of summer. On that note, we'll say the Pledge of Allegiance and then talk about your free-writing compositions, which I will return. A lot of you mentioned plans for the summer. I myself will be going to England to study Shakespeare."

"Good for you, Mr. Merrill," said Beth Ann. "I'm going to Disneyland!"

Shirley listened to others with lofty travel plans, holding the baseball glove in her lap and happily thinking about her own plan to go to Lake Winnipesaukee. Until the classroom door opened and there was Mrs. Greif, looking as elegant as ever in a cantaloupe-colored *chemise* (French for "shift"—say: "shuh-meez").

"See you all later," said Mr. Merrill to the class.

Mrs. Greif taught everyone summer words like: *soleil* ("sun"—say: "so-lay"), *plage* ("beach"—say: "plahzh"), *vacances* ("vacation"—say: "vah-cahnce"), and *été* ("summer"—say: *ay-tay*).

At the end she said, "This is our last French class together. Next year you will all have the option in your new schools to continue with French or to choose Spanish. How many of you will choose Spanish?"

Lannie Kaufman stuck up her hand immediately and said, "Me!" Cynthia Sparks put her hand up, too. Shirley was sure Cynthia was thinking about the rubber band she'd be shot with if she didn't agree with Lannie.

Shirley hoped Mrs. Greif wouldn't be offended. *"Au revoir,"* Madame Greif said ("Till I see you again"—say: "O reh-vwah").

Shirley wondered when that would be. Maybe never. Until she didn't wonder anymore because there was Mrs. Greif standing right beside her and asking a question.

"Would you help me start a French club this summer, Mademoiselle Shirley? I checked the school file for your address, and it seems we live so close to one another that you can walk to my apartment from your apartment. I live near Smilen Brothers! Remember, I will be going to Paris for the second two weeks in July. But I will be home after that."

147

"I'll have to ask my mother," Shirley answered, but already the wheels in her head were spinning. Forward.

Mrs. Greif wrote down her phone number on a piece of paper, which Shirley put in the pocket of her dress. And then Mrs. Greif and her very French perfume were gone, taking the time only to greet Mr. Merrill as they changed places.

Shirley watched as Mr. Merrill fiddled at his desk for a few minutes arranging papers, straightening books, opening a drawer, taking off his jacket, and then hanging it on the back of his chair. Shirley watched every move with her head down, but not her eyes. At any moment she expected Mr. Merrill to send her to the office. To tell her to forget about the rest of the school year—no prom for you—to express his disbelief that she dared insinuate that he'd made a mistake. Teachers don't make mistakes, Mr. Merrill would boom in front of the whole class. Eyes enraged. Nostrils flaring out like a dragon's. Crushing Shirley's valiant attempt to stick up for herself—in the name of justice—in an un-erasable letter that she had written in pen.

"While you were having the last French class of the year with Mrs. Greif," Mr. Merrill started, "I was meeting with the other sixth-grade teachers about the prom. It's all set for next Tuesday, the last day of school."

Shirley couldn't move except to shake, to sweat cold

everywhere a kid could sweat, and to feel the contents of her stomach sloshing around like clothes in a washing machine. *Has Mr. Merrill read my letter yet?* she asked herself. And then she knew the answer.

"Shirley," said Mr. Merrill, "please stay and talk to me before you join the others in the lunchroom."

When the last of the members of Class 6-1 filed out of the room, Mr. Merrill said, "I read your letter, Shirley. Twice, as a matter of fact. Clearly it was written straight from your heart."

He read it, Shirley thought, her face flushing who knew what color.

"I waited last Friday afternoon for you to tell me that your Listening Post essay was, in fact, your own, hoping you would defend yourself like any good writer would. But when you said nothing, I assumed your silence was an admission of guilt," Mr. Merrill said, kindly and with soft eyes. "I was wrong not to trust you, and I'm deeply sorry. Of course, it's too late to send your essay to WNYC, but I hope you will regard that essay as one of your finest accomplishments in sixth grade. It will be truly mean-ingful when you join the Peace Corps, which I have no doubt you will." Mr. Merrill stopped talking. He waited for Shirley to say something.

This time she did. "I'm sorry, too," she said. "I wanted to speak up. But I couldn't."

"Shirley Alice Burns, you have such a nice voice," said Mr. Merrill. "I hope you will let everyone hear it in junior high."

He said I have a nice voice, thought Shirley. Now that was something to hold on to.

Then she left the classroom to join the other kids at lunch.

Chapter 16
THE LAST SUPPER

TO CELEBRATE THE END OF SCHOOL, OR SO SHIRLEY THOUGHT, SHE
and Anna and Hal, but not Grandma, were going out for
dinner to the House of Wing, the best Chinese restaurant in Queens. Shirley wore her new hydrangea sundress, which Grandma had just finished sewing, and her
new sandals, which had only needed to be walked around
in for a couple of days with socks on until they were broken in.

Shirley twirled around in Grandma's latest creation.
Grandma reached over to adjust one of the straps. Anna
brushed Shirley's droopy eyebrows upward with her
fingers. Shirley, in turn, went into the Palace of Light.
She smiled at her reflection in the mirror. She liked what
she saw.

"Guess what, Mouse?" she whispered. "Shirley Alice

Burns has turned mountains of fear into molehills. She had the courage of her convictions to stand up to a teacher, of all people. Who knows what this girl will do next!"

When Hal beeped the horn, Grandma told Shirley, "Have a vonderful time!"

"I'll bring you a spare rib," Shirley promised.

"No, thank you," said Grandma.

Anna and Shirley left the apartment together. But Shirley stopped to talk to Luke.

"Congratulations, missy," he said.

"For what?" Shirley asked.

"Fer just about completin' the sixth grade," said Luke. "I was hopin' ta run into ye." Luke took a small yellow case out of one of the front pockets of his overalls.

"I got this fer ye," he said.

It was a set of screwdrivers: the smallest one was so small that Shirley could fix Grandma's unnecessary eyeglasses with it if a screw ever fell out. The biggest was the perfect size to fix the frying-pan handle if it ever came loose.

Shirley's smile would be enough for Luke, she knew, but she also said, "I really love it!" which made Luke smile, too. "I'm going to help you this summer, if that's okay, Luke," Shirley said, which made him smile even more broadly.

Anna might have had something to say about that, but Anna was already in Hal's van and didn't hear Shirley's offer.

Or Luke's answer. "Anytime at all, missy. Anytime at all."

· · · · ·

"Hiya, Skinny," said Hal when Shirley creaked open the passenger-side door.

Shirley assumed Anna had gotten the kiss she wanted; she looked happy. But Shirley got what she wanted, too: no kiss, because she was too far away on the long bench seat for Hal to reach. In front of the mannequin arms and legs and heads that were about to roll.

While they waited for their main courses at the House of Wing, Anna, Hal, and Shirley drank their exotic drinks and tasted different appetizers. Anna allowed Shirley to have ginger ale, which gave her hiccups. Their drinks had pink-and-yellow paper umbrellas in them that Shirley thought would be perfect for a diorama. They dipped noodles into a dish of sweet duck sauce, nibbled on spare ribs from the pupu platter, and slurped bowls of wonton soup. The *YCDBSOYA* tie clip helped Hal keep his tie out of the soup, but it didn't do anything about keeping the soup out of his mustache.

Shirley made an effort to look interested when Hal talked about espadrilles, the shoes every woman wanted for summer. Shirley felt herself beginning to soften just a little where Hal was concerned. At the very least, for Anna, who thought Hal was the man of her dreams. Shirley wanted Anna to stay happy because maybe then she would be nicer. Also the *YCDBSOYA* on Hal's tie clip had helped Shirley with Mr. Merrill.

Shirley excused herself to check out the opulent ladies' room, a Chinese Palace of Light. When she got back, their main courses had arrived, but Hal and Anna were engaged in a lively and smoky discussion and were not eating them. They stopped abruptly when Shirley sat down.

Hal reached to the right of his seat and handed Shirley a white shoebox with a new pair of Keds inside—to wear to camp, he said—and a book called *The Shirley Temple Storybook.* "For your birthday coming soon," Hal said. "She's a Shoiley like you're a Shoiley."

Shirley accepted the presents, only minding a little that Hal had signed his name on the inside of the book in ink: *From Hal to Shirley With Love.*

But then Anna started crying and holding on to Hal's hand.

"I am going to Baltimore to open a new shoe store called Halwyn's, because Hal wants to win, Shoiley, my goil," said Hal.

Shirley now understood the reason for Anna's tears.

"I know you and your ravishing mom and captivating grandma will get along capitally without me," Hal added with his usual largesse, this time of words.

After Hal's declaration, Anna and Shirley did not stay to eat the main course or the dessert or fortune cookies. They stayed for as long as Hal needed to pay the check. Anna's decision.

Shirley was truly shocked that Hal was absconding to Baltimore even though his demise had been one of her private hopes. She pretended to read "Rumpelstiltskin" in her new *Shirley Temple Storybook* at the table while Anna yelled, but she was actually thinking about some more reasons for remembering Hal: she would remember him for making her blood boil over the Big Daddy thing; for the words of the week he brought to dinner on Sundays, including *ravishing* and *captivating* and *capitally*; for letting her see the sweet side of Anna as someone's *amie* ("girlfriend" in French—say: "ah-me"); and for making Grandma speak Russian so much that Shirley learned many new words. Hal was pretty pivotal in all of their lives.

Grandma had been right about Hal, however. He had a secret: three of them, in fact. One wife and two children, who would be moving to Baltimore with him, which Hal had told Anna about at the restaurant—and which Anna told Shirley about in the taxi going home.

"And a lot of stolen shoes," Anna said, negating any largesse that Shirley thought Hal had displayed. Anna did not say: Smart Grandma. But Shirley thought it.

• • • • •

"I'll never forget Hal's tie clip," Shirley told Grandma on the couch that night.

"Vhat in the vorld are all those letters?" Grandma asked, braiding her hair.

Shirley wrote out the words on the back of a Larry's Taxicab Company envelope—You Can't Do Business Sitting On Your Apron—so that Grandma would understand better.

Shirley went outside. She swung around on the post that held up the roof over the stoop, assuring herself that she and Anna would be okay once Grandma moved. Shirley knew how to warm things up on the stove and cook if she had to, shop for things, wash dishes, and vacuum. She could do the laundry and would remember her key so she could get inside when she came home from school or from anywhere else. Shirley was thinking of the one thing she would not have—a dog—when Mr. Bickerstaff and Mustard came downstairs.

"You have a great dog, Mr. Bickerstaff," Shirley said, and then added, "In case you're interested, I would be happy to take Mustard to the park this summer while you are at work. It's so pretty there, and Mustard would love to run around with the other dogs and with me. I have a lot of experience from walking my aunt Claire's dog, Natalie."

"I'll pay you three dollars a week," said Mr. Bicker-staff, a dollar more than Shirley had been getting from Hal for her allowance.

Wait till I tell Phillie, she thought. *And Anna, who is not yet aware that I will have enough free time to walk Mustard since I won't be going to Breezy Bay Day Camp.* Shirley would even be able to buy her *own* bathing suit to take to Lake Winni Pee. She couldn't wait to tell Phillie about that either.

Chapter 17
THE PONY; THE TWIST; ONE, TWO, CHA-CHA-CHA

THE FIRST THING SHIRLEY SAW WHEN SHE ENTERED THE GYM THE following Tuesday with her class was a sweeping paper banner that said GOOD LUCK TO PS 606Q'S GRADUATING SIXTH GRADERS!

There were colored balloons with matching ribbons hanging from the basketball hoops, streamers on the lunchroom chairs, shiny silver and gold tablecloths on the lunchroom tables, and pictures of each sixth-grade class on the walls. All the men teachers were dressed up in jackets, some striped, some not, with festive ties. The women teachers wore spaghetti-strap dresses in hot summer colors. Shirley was elated to see Mrs. Greif modeling a silky salmon-colored French party dress, a French twist, and a pair of open-toed shoes exactly like Anna's.

Mrs. Greif always looked so cool, even when it was stifling.

"Bonjour, Madame!" Shirley said.

"Bonjour, Mademoiselle!" said Mrs. Greif.

When Shirley told Mrs. Greif that she would love to help with the French club (even though she hadn't yet told Anna), she got a big hug. Shirley did not know how to say *hug* in French but promised herself that she'd look it up when she got home—right before she told Anna about her summer plans: all of them. Mrs. Greif led Shirley to a table to taste one of the buttery butterfly cookies she'd made at home for the celebration.

"We'll learn to bake these this summer," she told Shirley.

Barry and Maury (who, as Shirley had predicted, was okay sharing her and the prom with Barry), in new pants and new shirts, with no ties, had followed Shirley like loyal puppies, hoping to taste one of Mrs. Greif's pastries, too. In fact, they hoped to taste everything the various teachers and parents had brought: blond brownies and Toll House cookies, Greek baklava (Shirley's favorite) and Italian cannoli, Oreos, Lorna Doones, Sugar Wafers, Twinkies, Ring Dings, Peppermint Patties (which made Shirley sneeze), and Devil Dogs; potato chips, pretzels, and of course Fritos; and Hawaiian Punch, ginger ale, Coke, and Pepsi, as well as cherry, grape, and orange sodas, to wash it all down.

This is some party! Shirley thought, not knowing the difference between a Ring Ding, a Devil Dog, and a Twinkie since Anna didn't allow them at home.

Then there was the music blasting from amplifiers alongside a big record player that Mr. Hoffmann, the music teacher, had made himself master of, much like Ed Sullivan on *The Ed Sullivan Show*. Shirley recognized songs she'd listened to on the radio.

She had never done the twist before (or any other dance except ballet), and it was scary to think of doing it in such a big public place like the gym, with a floor that went on for what seemed like miles. The endless floor had never bothered Shirley when she had gym there. But this was the prom, and she felt more than a little unsure of herself.

Shirley looked around and saw that she was among some of the best people: Mrs. Greif, Maury and Barry, Edie, and Benny, kids she had known since kindergarten, along with a handful of her former teachers, who stopped in to say goodbye and good luck to their former students. She noticed Mr. Merrill on the other side of the gym taking pictures of the festivities.

Then Shirley, in a fancy red Helen Katz prom dress,

danced the twist with Barry and Maury, Edie, Benny, and anyone else who wanted to join them.

Chubby Checker had a new record out called "Pony Time," and Sharon Levitt showed everyone how to do the pony when the twist was over. The new dance involved a sort of high gallop to the left and then one to the right, over and over. There were so many kids on the gym floor that Shirley was absorbed into the crowd of them.

Shirley danced the cha-cha with Edie since neither Barry nor Maury knew how to do it. (Anna had taught her one weekend on their living room floor with the rug rolled back, when Madame Macaroni was sidelined by an attack of appendicitis.) When the record finished, Edie and Shirley hugged each other. Edie would be going to sleepaway camp for the summer, along with a lot of other kids like Maury, then on to her neighborhood junior high, different from Shirley's. Shirley was wondering how she would ever see Edie again when she felt Barry tapping her on the shoulder.

"Show me how to do the cha-cha," he said.

So Shirley did. "One, two, cha-cha-cha," she whispered, just loud enough, stepping forward with her right foot, backward with her left, and then three steps together with both feet.

Surprisingly, Barry got the hang of it right away and

kept coming back for more whenever Mr. Hoffmann played a cha-cha like Ricky Nelson's "Travelin' Man" or "Itsy Bitsy Teenie Weenie Yellow Polkadot Bikini."

But Shirley would never forget the slow dance she had with Maury to "Will You Love Me Tomorrow," a song performed by an all-girl band that Mr. Hoffmann played at the end. Her left cheek against Maury's right cheek, her right hand in his left hand, her left hand on his right shoulder—just like Shirley had imagined it would be when she'd first heard there would be a prom.

"Tonight you're mine, completely. You give your love, so sweetly," Shirley sang with the record—in her head. She didn't know if you were supposed to talk when you slow-danced, so she didn't.

But Maury did. "This is what Beryl Abbie would say right now: 'Slowly but surely'"—*surely* said like *Shirley* instead of like "shoe-r-ly"—"'they danced at the prom on the very last day of sixth grade.'"

Shirley laughed, first because she couldn't help it and second because she was happy. Especially when her eye caught Barry slow-dancing with Marcy Bronson. Shirley thought it didn't matter who had asked whom.

Just before it was time to go home, all the teachers lined up to sing a made-up song like a quadruple barbershop quartet, swaying to the highs and lows of Mr. Hoffmann's recorder:

Down the road from A-lex-and-er's

Where the shopping lies,

Don't forget P.S. 606

When you're in junior high.

Then Mr. Hoffmann took the recorder away from his mouth and sang "Quuueeens" all by himself.

Everyone clapped and laughed, and some kids even cried as they wished each other great summers and exchanged addresses.

Shirley knew she would miss the friends she'd made—friends she might never see again, like Barry-the-Brain and Benny, but hopefully not Edie. She would probably even miss Mr. Merrill.

She heard him say, "Good luck, kid," as she filed out the door for the last time.

Shirley looked in the direction of the voice. "Thanks," she said.

What could be the reason for Mr. Merrill in my life? Shirley asked herself as she walked. Then she knew: *To make me stronger with words. With my voice.*

· · · · ·

"You can't dance at two veddings with one behind anyvay, so it's a good thing you're not going to camp this year," Grandma said when Shirley told her about Mrs. Greif's French club during the summer.

Shirley laughed and went on, "We're going to learn about the Louvre and the Palace of Versailles, read *The Little Prince* from beginning to end in English *and* in French, and learn to bake buttery French pastries and crusty *pain*" (French for "bread"—say a very clipped "pa," as in *pat*, with just a hint of an *n*). Shirley hugged Grandma. "Which reminds me," she said, gently breaking the embrace to find her French dictionary. "The word for *hug* in French is not easy to say: it is *étreinte*—say: 'long a-trant.'"

· · · · ·

Late that afternoon, Shirley walked to the bus stop to meet Anna on her way home from work, determined to tell her everything about her plans for the summer.

But first Anna asked, "Did you have a great time at the prom?"

Shirley had to answer. "Really great!" she said, with a few carefully chosen details thrown in, before she got to the heart of the matter. As they walked arm in arm toward the apartment, Shirley said, "Only losers go to day camp when they are twelve years old, like I will be when Breezy Bay starts in July, and I am not a loser."

"Who said you were a loser?" asked Anna.

"A loser can be implied," said Shirley. "It's how a person feels about herself. I am not going. And that's the end of that."

"Who died and left you boss?" asked Anna without alluding to anything specific.

But Shirley said, "You know who died," giving Anna a chance to finally address the big *dead* issue that stood between them.

But, of course, Anna didn't. She looked quickly at Shirley and then she looked away.

Anna thinks that I could not possibly know about my father being dead, thought Shirley. *Come on, Anna, don't be afraid. I can handle it. I have handled it. Be a big girl. Just say it: your father is dead.*

But Anna didn't.

Instead she said, "If you think you can loiter on the streets of Queens all summer, my darling daughter, when I am far away in Manhattan, then you have another think coming."

But Shirley was prepared. "I will not be loitering. I am going to help Mrs. Greif start a French club, assist Luke with the maintenance of Sparrowood Gardens, walk Mustard while Mr. Bickerstaff is at work, and watch Markie when Mrs. Goodman needs to catch up with herself or her laundry or window washing or dirty dishes, since there will no longer be a Hal on Sundays to give me my allowance. I will earn the money myself, like Phillie does."

Anna looked at Shirley and this time, she did not look away.

Shirley slowly counted to six to deliver the penultimate pièce de résistance while she had a rapt audience in Anna: "And I *am* going to Lake Winnipesaukee this year, too." Then the ultimate: "And *you* are going to the Royal Academy of Ballet from now on—not me. And if you want to sit in the bathroom to get ready for your class for thirty minutes, be my guest, because I am done with that, too."

Anna lit a Benson & Hedges. She took a detour, leading Shirley to the deserted playground and to the swings next to the clothesline, next to the No Ball Playing field, behind their bedroom window and Luke's apartment next door to the laundry room. Anna put her secondhand designer purse at the bottom of the slide. Each of them sat on a swing.

"Why didn't you tell me you didn't like ballet?" Anna asked.

"Because I was afraid to," said Shirley. "Like you are sometimes afraid to tell *me* things."

"When am I afraid?" asked Anna, ever the roiling hurricane. "Name one time."

That was all Shirley needed to launch her attack.

Even though she had only planned to talk to Anna about her summer activities, Shirley would not let this opportunity slip through the cracks of the ancient Sparrowood Gardens playground and into oblivion.

"You know exactly what I'm talking about," said Shirley. "You were afraid to tell me my father died because I was a little kid and you didn't know how to say *dead* so it wouldn't hurt. You let all those years go by without any explanation, thinking it would all go away." Shirley's throat did not close. "Well, I have news for you: Sad news hurts. And if it doesn't, then there is something missing right here." Shirley put her hand over her heart.

"Who told you he died?" Anna asked.

"I opened the Larry's Taxicab letter last week," Shirley confessed. "I didn't understand what most of it said— except for the deceased part."

"I can explain," said Anna. "Uncle Bill encouraged me to bring a lawsuit against Larry's Taxicab Company because your father had a heart attack and an accident on the job. Or an accident and then a heart attack. Uncle Bill thinks I am entitled to some compensation as the wife. But it is taking a long, long time to sort out." Then Anna added, "When my ship comes in, you and I will take a nice vacation. Maybe to the Pocono Mountains. And I am sorry you had to find out that way."

"I am okay with knowing," Shirley said. "In fact, I am

more okay now than when I waited by the curb all those Wednesdays for my father to come. And I felt so empty when I had to go back upstairs alone, thinking he didn't love me anymore."

"Shirley," said Anna. "My girl."

"Knowing things, even terrible things, makes you tougher," continued Shirley. "It's important to know everything you can so you understand your own life."

Anna's nose was turning red. A plain weepy, splotchy red. Not pretty red like Shirley's slow-dancing prom dress. Anna wiped her nose, her eyes, her cheeks. Shirley came over to Anna's swing and sat in her lap; she put her right arm around Anna's back, and held the chain of the swing with her left hand, both feet on the ground, rocking the swing gently back and forth like a cradle. *Who ever heard of an almost-twelve-year-old sitting on her mother's lap?* Shirley wondered. Then she thought, *Who cares?*

"Your father loved you," said Anna. "But I didn't love your father."

Quite suddenly, though Shirley had never wanted to tell Anna about her trouble with Mr. Merrill, she decided to tell her now. Shirley got off Anna's lap and returned to the other swing, where she blurted out everything. To prove to Anna that she was not the kid she used to be. The kid that Anna thought she still was. That she—Shirley Alice

Burns—had recently handled a very hard situation all by herself.

Anna's perfect-lipstick mouth dropped open at the beginning and stayed that way until Shirley had finished.

"You would never plagiarize anything," said Anna, scraping her espadrilles on the ground. "I'll cripple him," she added, exaggerating as only Hurricane Anna could. "Why didn't you tell me?"

"That's why," said Shirley, standing up. "You would have made it a gargantuan deal and not let me fix the problem myself."

"It *is* a gargantuan deal," said Anna.

She sat as still in the swing as Shirley had ever seen her mother sit.

Shirley was immensely relieved that the Mr. Merrill secret was out. She hoped Anna would get it: Get Shirley Alice Burns for the first time in both of their lives. Get that Shirley needed to stand up on her own two feet— and that Anna needed to let go.

But then Anna surprised her by saying, "Just think of all the money we'll save if you don't take ballet."

"Not if *you* take ballet with Madame Macaroni," said Shirley.

"Very funny," said Anna.

"Why can't you?" Shirley asked.

"I meant very funny about her name," said Anna.

Shirley had forgotten that no one knew about Madame Macaroni's alias except for her.

"And just think of all the money we'll save if you don't go to Breezy Bay Day Camp," said Anna.

"Do you mean it?" asked Shirley.

"I mean it," said Anna.

On the way back to their apartment, Shirley said, "I'm sorry about Hal."

"I know you are," said Anna.

Anna sang "Hit the Road, Jack!" like Ray Charles all the way home from the playground, which Shirley interpreted to mean: Good riddance, Hal. I will be okay without you.

When they got home, Grandma said, "I vas going to send a search party to look for you two. Then I looked from the bedroom vindow and I saw you vere on the svings."

· · · · ·

After dinner, Anna took to cleaning furiously. Shirley supposed she missed Hal more than she let on.

It had been a good day. A lucky day. But it wasn't over yet. When Shirley brought the trash over to the garbage house, a few of the kids were already there. Not for tag-around-the-garbage-house as Shirley had expected, but for something else.

"We're going to play spin the bottle tonight," said Monica Callahan. "You're invited, Shirley." Monica showed Shirley the empty cream-soda bottle she'd been hiding behind her back.

"Am I invited?" asked Beryl Abbie.

"Sorry, Beryl Abbie," said Monica, being uncharacteristically sensitive to the small girl's feelings. "You're not old enough."

· · · · ·

There were six of them seated in a circle on the cool, dry floor in the dimmest corner of the laundry room: Monica Callahan, Dale Rosenberger, Maury Gordon, Curtis Karl, Laurence-with-a-*u* Livingstone, and Shirley Alice Burns. Shirley's stomach fluttered like feathers in front of a fan.

"Does everyone know how to play?" asked Monica.

Shirley was glad that Edie had explained the rules to her so she wouldn't draw attention to her unworldly self. But when Maury admitted that he didn't know how to play, Shirley was glad to hear the rules again.

"If Dale spins the bottle like this," said Monica, demonstrating how to do it, "then she gets to kiss the boy closest to the nose of the bottle—Laurence in this case. Or she can kiss the girl closest to where the nose of the bottle stops."

"No thanks," said Dale. Everyone knew that Dale liked Curtis and would rather kiss him.

Now Shirley's stomach felt as wavy as Jones Beach on a stormy day. She wished she hadn't eaten so much spaghetti for dinner. *I want to be here,* she thought. *I have wanted to do this for so long.* She pushed her stomach in with two hands. Maury sat to her left, Curtis to her right. It was boy, girl, boy, girl, boy, girl. Six former sixth graders in all.

Shirley got to kiss all the boys that night, but it was Maury's kiss that meant the most: warm and soft like the inside of one of Grandma's buttermilk biscuits.

Chapter 18
CHILDREN WITH PUG NOSES

ANNA, EITHER BY CHANCE OR ON PURPOSE, HAD LEFT HER eighth-grade autograph album in the Palace of Light on the shelf with the matches, Shirley noticed when she got home that night. If the second of the two situations was the case, and Anna actually wanted her to read the little book, Shirley was more than happy to oblige.

Shirley was flush with the thrill of the recent clandestine experience she'd just shared with the five other Sparrowood Gardens kids, especially Maury, filled with the fun she'd had at the prom, the pride of graduating from P.S. 606Q, and the excitement of looking ahead to a summer like no other summer she had ever looked ahead to before.

"Who could be luckier than I am, Mouse?" Shirley asked. "No one."

Shirley eagerly opened the small leather autograph book in the privacy of the Palace of Light, saying, "Here we go!"

The first thing Shirley noticed was the exemplary cursive writing—even from the boys. Not true for everyone in *her* class. The second thing she noticed was that the girls who'd autographed Anna's album wrote mostly about boys and love and marriage and babies, while the boys wrote silly things upside down and crooked just to be remembered. To leave their marks on history.

Shirley wondered why the girls couldn't be silly, too. In any case, she hoped she would find something about Anna's boyfriend if she'd had one then. Maury was going off to Camp Eureka, a science camp, for an entire month. Maybe he wouldn't even want to be her boyfriend when he came back.

Inside the album, Anna's name was glittered in gold, *Anna Botkin*, along with the school she went to, *P.S. 20, the Bronx*. Shirley imagined that Anna liked glittering the numbers and letters as much as she liked polishing her nails now.

Shirley flipped to the beginning. After Anna wrote about reading this autograph book in her old age, which she apparently had just done, there was a page on which the principal of Anna's school had written: *To the sweetest girl in the world, you have changed my attitude toward life.* What had Anna done, Shirley wondered, to inspire him to write that? Maybe Anna answered the phone in the school office in a loud and clear voice, like she did at Mr. Joseph's, and always knew what to say when people asked questions like "How many grades are there at P.S. 20?"

Anna: "There are eight. Thank you for calling."

Shirley felt validated when she read the parts in Anna's album that described Anna exactly as Shirley knew her:

> Anna, Anna loves to bite
> Better yet, she loves to fight
> She's so mean, but yet despite
> I love her with all my might.

Shirley liked this one, too:

> New York girls are pretty
> New York girls are nice
> But when it comes to Anna
> Hot dog! She cracks the ice!

And this one:

> May your path be strewn with roses
> And your children have pug noses
> Yours till a mountain peaks
> And sees a salad dressing.

This is what Shirley found out from reading Anna's autograph book: Anna was once a girl like her and Pippi Longstocking and Astrid Lindgren. She got into trouble, kissed some boys, tried her best in school, played hard at recess, was afraid of things, laughed a lot, and maybe even had a big dream like Shirley did of the Peace Corps. It didn't say if Anna cried or not, but then Shirley didn't cry much either.

This is what Shirley concluded: *I guess Anna must have been around long enough for me to get her genes. When Grandma moves, and Anna and I are on our own, I may have to be the voice of reason, even if Anna won't listen. And I am more than ready to be pugnacious.*

Chapter 19
THE REASON FOR MOVING

THE FOLLOWING SATURDAY, SHIRLEY HEARD GRANDMA SAYING
goodbye to the white ceramic dog, the heart picture
frame, and the aqua-colored doll chair, among other
things.

"I have no vindowsill in my new apartment," said
Grandma, "so you can keep all these pretty things, Shirley, my sunny child."

"Okay," said Shirley. "And when you come over, you
can visit them."

Because she didn't own a suitcase, Grandma packed
her life into seven Macy's shopping bags: her clothes,
shoes, coats, whatever sewing and knitting things she
had (needles, bobbins, thread, yarn, buttons, scissors,
dress material), and three entire bags of hardcover
books along with their dust jackets, which Grandma had

indeed hidden under her couch-bed as Shirley had suspected.

"If you ever need anything, tell me," Grandma told Shirley. "I vould give you my life."

Shirley stuck to the front of Grandma's polka-dot cotton dress, filling her nose, her eyes, her skin, and her heart with Grandma, knowing how precious a life was.

Grandma kissed Anna goodbye. "Be okay," she said to her in Russian.

"You, too," said Anna.

Luke moved the seven Macy's shopping bags, one sewing machine, and one Grandma in his light blue Ford Falcon. Shirley went along for the ride.

"Ye can call me day or night, Granny," said Luke, "whenever ye're needing help."

"I vill," Grandma promised.

To say thank you, Grandma gave Luke a jar of apricot jam that she'd made from apricots on the tree she'd planted more than six years ago in the garden outside their Sparrowood Gardens apartment.

· · · · ·

Shirley loved Grandma's new apartment. It had furniture and dishes that had been stored in Aunt Rosalie's garage from her Grandpa days, pillows and rugs from Aunt Claire's basement, and pots and pans and silverware that Grandma bought new from Macy's. It even had a small garden out front that caught the warm rays of the afternoon sun like Grandma's garden in Sparrowood had. Uncle Rod, Steve, and Phillie had delivered and organized everything the day before so that Grandma's move would be as easy for her as it could be. Everyone in the family knew that Grandma had never lived alone in her entire life. And everyone wanted her new place to feel homey on the very first day.

. . . . .

Later that afternoon, back at home, Shirley started working on a new diorama before she and Anna had to get ready to go to Aunt Claire's for Saturday-night dinner. They had arranged to pick up Grandma on their way and walk together as if nothing had changed.

On the wood part of the bedroom floor, Shirley cut out a rectangle from an old white Christmas box to make a block of attached houses. She colored each house terracotta red and with a ruler drew straight black horizontal lines and small vertical lines to denote the bricks. Shirley carefully cut out windows and doors that opened, and pasted a smiling paper girl on a paper bicycle with hand-brakes and a big basket to carry library books and groceries. She took a long time to get the girl and the bicycle to stand upright, using tape and strips of cardboard attached to the gray paper sidewalk in front of the houses. Shirley was just drawing a yellow paper dog when the phone rang.

Anna said a loud "Hello" into the receiver. And then she didn't say another word for so long that Shirley found herself stopping what she was doing and going into the kitchen, hoping the news wasn't half as bad as Anna's face said it was when she hung up.

There had been a fire. An electrical fire. In the walls. Of the basement. Of the Barretts' disorganized brick attached house. While the Barrett kids and Aunt Rosalie were out getting their short Lake Winnipesaukee haircuts at Sal's Barbershop on Main Street. The fire burned the walls in the basement. It ate the floor, the ceiling, and Uncle Rod's recliner. It melted the washing machine, exploded the Zenith TV, and burned all the games and the books and the toys on the shelves and in the toy chest. It reduced Phillie's road racing table, his road racing set, and his remaining stash of cash in the cardboard saltwater taffy bank to ashes. And it killed Harry the piranha.

"Can you believe it, Mouse?" Shirley asked, stunned.

"An electrical fire. Which no one was at home to stop or to call the fire department about."

· · · · ·

"Harry couldn't run up the stairs to the bedroom like Porky did to save himself," Phillie said, sobbing into his handkerchief when Shirley, Anna, and Grandma got to Aunt Claire's. "So he died."

Of course, the fire was the only subject of conversation at the dinner table.

"Thank God no vone vas home," said Grandma.

Everyone nodded.

"The fire destroyed the kitchen. Turned all the appliances from green to black," said Aunt Rosalie, while Uncle Rod sat and listened, holding on to Porky's collar so he wouldn't eat the beef stroganoff that Aunt Claire had just placed on the fancy Saturday-dinner tablecloth. Shirley saw Uncle Rod shake his head as if to say: How could this have happened to us?

"You should see the piles of ashes," said Ruthie.

"All our stuff is sooty and charred, and it stinks like smoke," said Laurel. "Our beds and clothes and dolls and shoes. Even our school pictures."

"We can't sleep in our own house," said Steve. "It doesn't have any windows anymore."

"So let's sleep at Winnipesaukee!" said Scott.

Aunt Rosalie did not say, "Who asked you?" because she may have thought Scott had a good idea. Or maybe she couldn't bring herself to say, "There will be no Winnipesaukee this year, kids." Shirley couldn't tell. The room was already overflowing with sadness; no one could add any more. No *hahahas* came from Aunt Rosalie tonight. Only tears.

Shirley sat in the chair next to Phillie, thinking about the different kinds of grief there were in the universe, and how terrible each one was to the person experiencing it. She would have easily given up her best wish—to go to Lake Winnipesaukee—to reverse the tragedy of that afternoon, just so the fire would not have destroyed the Barretts' house. Fizzled before it started. Changed its mind. Was put out by a sudden, heavy downpour.

Conflagration was a big word for "fire." It was the same word in French, but with a French accent. Shirley hated that word and refused to say it. *I will never light another conflagration in the sink in the Palace of Light ever again,* she promised.

· · · · ·

"I'm so sorry, Phillie," Shirley said, her arm around Phillie's quivering shoulders as they walked Natalie and

Porky down to the park after dinner. Porky was attached to one of Natalie's rhinestone leashes since his leash had been lost in the fire.

"At least you have fire insurance, so you guys can get all new things."

"I guess," said Phillie. "Dad says we might get air conditioners in every room."

But they both knew without saying that no fire insurance could ever replace Harry.

. . . . .

"So did Natalie do her big business?" Aunt Claire asked when Shirley brought Natalie back.

"Nope, she didn't. Not today," said Shirley, looking right into Aunt Claire's big, scary eyes. Without flinching.

It was decided that Aunt Rosalie and Uncle Rod and Steve and Scott and Porky would stay at Aunt Claire and Uncle Bill's house. Grandma took Laurel and Ruthie home to her new apartment, happy to help—happy for the company in her cozy quarters. Phillie went home with Shirley. Anna invited him to sleep on the couch that had just been vacated by Grandma.

"Until your house is ready to be lived in again, sweetheart," she said. "You are welcome to stay for the whole summer."

Maybe Hurricane Anna was finally weakening. Blowing out to sea. Shirley certainly hoped so.

"Let's play train before we go to bed," Shirley said to Phillie. "You can decide where we go, and I won't argue. Come and help me carry the box down from the high dresser."

But when Shirley and Phillie went into the bedroom and looked up, the big brown box was not there. It had been replaced by a silver mermaid.

"Where are my trains?" Shirley asked Anna. "Where did you move them?"

It was then that Anna admitted she had given Shirley's beloved Lionel train set to Scott only the day before. The big carton had been picked up by Uncle Rod, after yet another all-out cleaning of their apartment by Anna.

"I thought the top of the dresser was the perfect spot for the mermaid I just polished the other day," said Anna.

Shirley glared resentfully at the haughty mermaid.

"I didn't think you still played with those trains," Anna continued. "I thought they were just something else that needed to be dusted."

Anna is so oblivious to important things, thought Shirley, remembering well the last time she and Maury set up the tracks in the bedroom while Anna was busy on the phone in the kitchen. Hadn't she heard the *choo-choos*?

"That must have been the box my dad put under the road racing table in the basement," said Phillie, "as soon as we got back from Grandma's apartment."

Anna covered her face with both hands, seemingly filled with genuine remorse, while Phillie cried again over one more thing that had been lost in the fire.

Since they couldn't play train, Shirley and Phillie watched *Tarzan* on Channel 9 until their eyes began to close. It happened that *Tarzan* was one of Phillie's favorite movies.

Phillie chose to sleep in his clothes that night because he had nothing else to sleep in except for his underwear, which he didn't want everyone to see. He brought his pillow and blanket into Anna and Shirley's bedroom and asked if he could sleep on the floor so they would all be cooled off by the fan in the window and because he was so used to sharing a room with two other people that he didn't think he could fall asleep without someone snoring.

"I will try to make you feel right at home," said Anna, who had been told on more than one occasion by Shirley that she snored like a bear.

"Did you tell Mouse what happened?" Phillie whispered,

half-asleep, when Anna turned the other way and began breathing heavily.

"Yeah," said Shirley. "I did."

"What did he say?" Phillie asked, lifting his head from the pillow.

"He said not to worry. You'll live," said Shirley. "And he said he was really sorry."

• • • • •

That night Shirley dreamed she was being chased by hostile jungle people like the ones Tarzan and Jane met up with in the movie. As Shirley ran her fastest, she desperately tried to grab on to one of the many overhanging vines that appeared to be too high for her to reach. And when she finally did catch one, she struggled mightily to shimmy up, as scared as she'd ever been in her entire life, knowing all too well that pull-ups had never been her best unit in gym at P.S. 606Q. But with her unfaltering determination Shirley, in her dream, made it to the very top of the vine in the end. When she'd swung her legs over the edge of the ledge she realized, with great relief, that she was in, of all places, heaven.

"That was close!" said Shirley when she woke up, all of her covered in sweat.

"What was close?" asked Phillie.

Shirley told him about her dream.

"I think you're scared to be away from home for the first time when we go to Lake Winni Pee," he said. "If we're still going."

"We're going," said Shirley, trying to sound upbeat for Phillie's sake.

Then Phillie said, "Who asked you?" and they both burst out laughing.

· · · · ·

That day, while Phillie and Shirley were outside playing catch with the blue ball on the No Ball Playing field, taking turns with Shirley's new baseball glove, Maury came over with his own glove, his brother's glove, and a real baseball. Then the three of them tossed the baseball around instead of the blue ball. Shirley loved the pounding sound the baseball made as it worked itself into the pocket of the leather glove. Phillie's glove, of course, had been roasted to a crisp by the fire.

"When's camp?" Shirley asked Maury.

"Day after the Fourth of July—Wednesday," said Maury.

"Are you excited?" Shirley asked.

"Yeah," said Maury, adding, "I know my camp address by heart. Want it?"

"Sure," said Shirley.

"Can I have it, too?" asked Beryl Abbie. She had seen Maury from her window and couldn't resist coming out to see him.

So Maury told Shirley his camp address, which she easily memorized because it was so simple: Maury Gordon, Camp Eureka, Liberty, New York. Then Maury recited it again for Beryl Abbie, who had gone home to get a pen because she wasn't good at memorizing addresses, only songs. She wrote it all down on the palm of her hand because she had forgotten to bring paper.

"You can borrow the baseball if you want," Maury told Shirley. "We'll play when I get back from camp in August."

There was no mention of the fire. If Maury had heard about it, Shirley figured, he probably knew in his heart that Phillie didn't want to be reminded over and over about something as terrible as that fire.

Then Anna called out to Shirley and Phillie from the bedroom window to come in and get ready to go shopping for some new pajamas, shorts, and shirts to tide Phillie over until he could collect his smoky clothes from the smoky bedroom that he shared with Steve and Scott.

Anna, Phillie, and Shirley walked over to catch the bus to Queens Boulevard. Then they hailed a taxi to Alexander's Department Store, down the road from P.S. 606Q. Shirley looked at the schoolyard from the taxi window. She smiled.

"I got the deposit back from Breezy Bay Day Camp yesterday," said Anna, "so we can splurge! And I have my vacation pay besides."

Anna's vacation had always been the same: the first two weeks in July. Her vacation of choice had always been the same, too: a trip to Lake Layaway. Shirley knew she would have to take matters into her own hands to get Anna to start contributing to her Attached House Fund until Anna's ship came in. Whenever that would be.

"I'll wash all your smoky clothes for you when you get them from your house, Phillie," said Shirley, seated between Anna and Phillie in the taxi. "Then I'll hang them outside so they'll smell really fresh—I'm an expert, you know—and you can sing with Beryl Abbie on the swings."

"I can't wait," said Phillie.

Without being asked, Anna bought Shirley a new bathing suit. Shirley chose blue. And as a special treat, she got Phillie and Shirley goggles from the five-and-ten-cent store on Queens Boulevard, after she heard Phillie mention the demise of his green ones in the fire.

Shirley suspected Anna's generosity might be a clue to the Winnipesaukee trip: that it was still on. Maybe Anna knew something that she and Phillie didn't. Shirley hoped so. She wanted to believe that Anna had given Aunt Rosalie and Uncle Rod the okay—and wanted Shirley to be surprised when she found out.

"Does this mean we're still going?" Shirley whispered.

"What do you mean *we*?" Phillie asked, wrinkling his brow, trying to look sinister, trying to be contrary.

Shirley loved the excitement all over Phillie's face because this year, if the trip was still on, she would be going, too.

. . . . .

When Luke heard about the fire, he offered to help Phillie build a new road racing table.

"I happen to have lots of extra pieces of wood left over from various projects around Sparrowood," Luke said. "I'll be glad to let ye have them fer yer table. Maybe I can even have me own racing car!"

Phillie knew Luke was kidding. But he said anyway, "It's a deal!"

Shirley loved sanding the wood and hammering the nails. Luke let Phillie try his electric saw. Shirley said, "I'd rather not," when Luke held the saw out to her.

· · · · ·

When Shirley's twelfth birthday arrived on July 6th, Uncle Rod drove everyone to Palisades Amusement Park in New Jersey. Because that's where Shirley wanted to go. Shirley thought the Barrett kids could use some fun. She thought everyone could use some fun. Grandma went, too, and rode a white horse on the little kids' merry-go-round, her fat legs barely reaching the stirrups, her smile wide every time she came around to where Shirley was watching. Anna rode the roller coaster like she always told Shirley she had at Coney Island—probably, Shirley thought, when she was that eighth-grade daredevil girl, that girl in the autograph album whom everybody loved.

It was on the way home that Uncle Rod informed everyone that he and Aunt Rosalie had decided that the long-anticipated trip to Lake Winnipesaukee was a definite *go*. "The timing couldn't be more perfect," he said, "since our house has a bunch of strangers in it anyway." He meant the construction people.

Then he added, winking at Shirley in the rearview mirror, "Do you think I'd pass up a chance to spend a couple of weeks on my favorite lake with my favorite niece?"

Shirley's cheeks turned carnation pink with delight.

With mild cheers of her own, Anna joined the wild cheers that filled the car.

When they got home, it was Shirley's turn to give Phillie a present. She'd paid for it with money she'd taken out of her Attached House Fund. The present was a brand-new Aurora Road Race set with the same extra cars they had chosen before the fire: a Batmobile for Phillie and a silver Corvette for her. There was a third car, too: a Ferrari for Luke. There would be a time one day, she thought, when they could set up the tracks and cars in the storage room before Phillie's new basement would be finished— when Luke could play, too. Shirley had ridden her bike to Wainwright's Department Store the day before, when Phillie went home to get his clothes. She carried the box on her handlebars in a giant Macy's shopping bag, pedaling slower than a tortoise could walk.

"If I had my stash of cash," said a very surprised Phillie, "I would have bought you a year's supply of Good & Plenty for your birthday."

Before Phillie could cry again at the thought of all the things he'd lost in the fire, Shirley reassured him. "Knowing you, your stash will be built up again in no time, just like your house," she said.

• • • • •

"I got the idea from Pippi," Shirley told Mouse while she packed her bag for Lake Winni Pee. "In the chapter

192

called 'Pippi Celebrates Her Birthday,' Pippi gives her friends presents because she says she should be allowed to do whatever she wants to on her birthday."

Then she told Mouse: "I hope you'll be okay under the Birds Eye frozen spinach while I'm away on vacation. I'll be doing everything for two, you know: you and me. I absolutely can't wait!"

Chapter 20
SMILING BACK AT THE GREAT SPIRIT

IT WAS A MID-JULY MORNING CROWNED BY SO MUCH SUNSHINE
that the dewdrops on the grass gleamed like diamonds as
Shirley and Phillie stepped all over them to get to the Barretts' station wagon which, at seven o'clock, was already
waiting by the curb. *The Palace of Light is outside today*,
thought Shirley as Aunt Rosalie asked from the front seat,
"Got your toothbrush and bathing suit, Shirley girl?" and
Phillie, running to the back of the car, lifted the big window of the trunk and flopped over onto the pillows, joining
Steve and Scott, who were already sprawled out.

Anna kissed Shirley on top of her head before asking
if she had remembered her Ivory soap, bathing cap, and
insect repellent.

Shirley took the seat by the window next to Laurel,
who along with Ruthie had been walked over by Grandma,

and stuffed her duffel bag under her legs. Uncle Rod wore his Bermuda shorts, summer driving cap, and big grin as he told Anna he would take good care of Shirley. Shirley waved goodbye to Anna and then to Grandma.

"Be okay," Grandma said in Russian, using the plural form of the verb to include everyone in the car.

•　•　•　•　•

Shirley felt nothing at first. Then she felt everything. She felt free. Free to be on her own in the big, big world. And she felt enclosed. Enclosed in the best way, when you belong somewhere. Somewhere like in the middle of the happy chaos that was the Barrett family.

No one was wearing the shirts that said all their names, Ruthie volunteered, because they'd been in the washing machine when the fire occurred. Shirley felt guilty, but she had to admit that she wasn't very sorry for that particular loss. When Aunt Rosalie said, "Who asked you?" in answer to Ruthie's announcement, Shirley found herself asking Ruthie the same.

Shirley tore napkins in half when they ate lunch and counted out ten M&M's for dessert so no one would get any more than anyone else. She felt like a kid. And she felt like a grown-up to be away from home and to love it so much. At first Shirley didn't think she mattered in such a big family of which she wasn't an immediate part. And then she felt like she did matter when Uncle Rod asked what radio station was her favorite (the rock-and-roll one, of course).

Here I am, mountains! Shirley thought when she first saw them from the car window, looking exactly like the little florets of broccoli that Aunt Rosalie described in last year's postcard. And the lake! The size of it: three hundred miles! The color *was* azure! Everything was azure! Every ounce of Shirley's being was filled with wonder.

"I never thought that I, Shirley Alice Burns, that mousy girl who keeps a mouse in the freezer in her apartment in Queens, would ever be lucky enough to be here! Can you see me, Mouse?" Shirley asked, mouthing the words.

There was cold, clean water to jump into from a wooden dock! A blue canoe to row with Phillie! And pretty blue-shuttered cabins around the lake to sleep in! *You can hear crickets all night like in the movies! And you don't even need a fan to keep cool because it is always cool here at night!* Shirley thought.

• • • • •

One day, Uncle Rod rented a motorboat and let Shirley hold the steering wheel. She loved the misty wind in her face, which made her curly hair even curlier. Shirley squealed with the other Barretts when they got splashed from the big waves the boat made.

When Uncle Rod killed the motor, Scott shouted: "Go jump in the lake!" And Shirley did.

They took pictures! And made a family movie! Shirley went camping for the first time and peed in the woods. *You're not the only one to do it outside, Monica Callahan!* Shirley thought.

Eating Cheerios in their pretty cabin with the blue shutters on the blue lake in her blue bathing suit, Shirley warned Phillie in a loud whisper, "Don't drink the milk."

"Why?" he asked, a wide grin breaking out all over his face.

"It's spoiled," said Shirley, as happy as she had ever been in her entire life.

She and Phillie laughed like two silly hyenas when Uncle Rod asked: "Why shouldn't I drink the milk?"

And Aunt Rosalie answered, "Who asked you?"

· · · · ·

Another day they rode a real train up the mountain. The only train Shirley had ever been on was the New York City subway—the E and F trains from Queens Boulevard were both underground. Now she and Phillie sat side by side in a small red flatcar for two that chugged along, slowly but steadily, up the steep mountainside.

"Look down!" said Phillie.

And Shirley did. But she was only half as scared as she had been when she went on Tony's Death-Defying Sky Ride with all the neighborhood kids—too chicken to sit in the top row and have her feet swinging in midair.

· · · · ·

Shirley tried waterskiing. She couldn't stand up on the skis the first time.

"Try again!" said Uncle Rod.

And fishing: "Blech!" said Shirley at the thought of fooling a fish to bite onto a sharp hook.

"It's good to know what you don't like," said Uncle Rod.

"Do I have to do it?" Phillie asked, no doubt thinking of poor Harry.

"Do *you* think you have to?" asked Uncle Rod.

And Phillie said quietly, "No."

Shirley thought Anna would have made Phillie go fishing. At least the old Anna would have. Who knew about the new Anna?

But Steve and Scott and Laurel loved fishing. And so did Uncle Rod.

Shirley thought of Grandma's five fingers: See them! They are all different! Smart Grandma.

Perhaps Shirley's favorite thing of all was floating on Lake Winnipesaukee under the sun, under the sky, in the water, on the earth; feeling the Smile of the Great Spirit; and smiling back. *The Smile of the Great Spirit is enormous like the lake,* Shirley thought. She was surprised she didn't have to look as hard to find it as she had at first imagined: under a boulder, at the bottom of the lake, in the fog, in the smoke coming from a special pipe. The Spirit was everywhere. You are okay as you are in the world today, it told Shirley; you will be okay for as long as you are alive. There is a reason for you.

Without intending to, Shirley felt the father whom she hadn't been allowed to feel, whom she hadn't been allowed to call anything—not even Dad: he was in the whistle she made with a blade of grass held tightly between her thumbs, in the beads of water on her knees, in the moving clouds that hovered above her head, in the sparrow that thought he was hidden in a sugar maple tree. "I see you," said Shirley. She felt her father's breath in a breeze; she smelled his aftershave when she walked past an evergreen.

One night she saw a bat circling in a field of foxtails and thought her father might have something to do with that bat; she heard her father laugh, like he did when she used to muss his hair, when she saw a misspelled word on a sign at a restaurant: DINNERS WELCOME! instead of DINERS WELCOME! Her father must have been a good speller, too, decided Shirley. She got his message when there was lightning during a storm over their cabin one afternoon: be strong, Shirley Burns.

·　·　·　·　·

Shirley sent postcards.

Hi Maury,

I went into the water on the front of this postcard and I got all wet! I think this place is better than heaven, since no one knows exactly what heaven is. How's that for science?

I put everything they had at Kellerhaus on my huge strawberry sundae (they didn't have pistachio) and ate every bit—until I had to drink the ice cream at the end. And it all only cost a dollar! I hope you like your camp. I LOVE LAKE WINNIPESAUKEE!

See you soon,
Shirley Alice Burns (in case you didn't know!)

Dear Edie,

Greetings from moi! (Remember our French?)
I'm having the best time ever at Lake
Winnipesaukee! I'll call you when I get
home so we can meet halfway on Queens
Boulevard.

S. A. B.

Dear Mom,

I've been swimming, canoeing, waterskiing, and
camping. I even rode a train up a giant
mountain. It is nicer here than in the picture!
Miss you.

Love,
Shirley

Shirley didn't write *Wish you were here* on Anna's postcard, because she didn't.

Dear Grandma,

Everything is blue here, except me. I am soooooo happy! You have to come next year!

Love and kisses,
Your sunny child, Shirley

And the last one to Luke in his basement apartment next to the laundry room:

Dear Luke,

I hope you are having a good summer so far. I am. I will tell you all about it when I get home. And by the way, I need to talk to you. It's about a funeral for a mouse.

Yours truly,
Shirley Burns
Apartment 6961A

Chapter 21

LUKE TO THE RESCUE

IT WASN'T THAT ANNA GOT A SUDDEN URGE FOR SPINACH. "I AVOID spinach like the plague," she always said. It was more that the refrigerator stopped refrigerating and Anna smelled something putrid when she opened the freezer door to investigate—and followed her nose to the *souris* (French for "mouse"—say: "soo-ree") in the checkbook box in the defrosted freezer.

"Shirley! Get this monster out of here!" Anna shrieked, as she was in the habit of doing in a frightful situation. But Shirley wasn't there this time to drop everything and race into the kitchen at breakneck speed to remove the monster because she was far away at Lake Winnipesaukee. Having the vacation of her dreams.

When Shirley got back (Phillie would join them later after checking on the progress of his house with his family), Anna and Grandma were there to greet her with lots of lingering kisses and unbreakable hugs, as if Shirley had been away for a year.

Then Anna demanded an explanation for the mouse in the freezer.

First Shirley said: "You didn't throw him away, did you?"

"No," Anna said. "I learned my lesson with your trains."

"I found him on Father's Day lying in the grass," Shirley said. "I picked him up, brought him home, and put him in the freezer so he would be there for as long as I needed him to be there—until I could understand about my father. Who happens to be as dead as that mouse. I wanted to know what dead was, and about some other things besides. And now I know. I'm glad you didn't take my mouse to the garbage house or flush him down the toilet."

"You're welcome," said Anna.

"So where is he?" asked Shirley.

"He's in the freezer of the new refrigerator that Luke brought over," said Anna.

"It isn't good to refreeze vhat has already been defrosted," said Grandma.

Anna glared at Grandma because she had, of course, refrozen the mouse.

"And, by the vay, I made some hamburgers and buttermilk biscuits vith American cheese to velcome you home, Shirley! You made Vinnipesaukee sound so good, my sunny child!" said Grandma.

Some things will always remain the same, like arguing over silly things like defrosting and refreezing, Shirley thought, *when there are more important things in the world to concern yourself with.*

On the way home in the Barretts' car, Shirley had planned a funeral for Mouse. For her father. A proper send-off to wherever the mouse body would be going next. She told Phillie there would be a funeral, but she didn't know when it would be.

• • • • •

Late in the day on Sunday, Shirley found Luke in the playground replacing the rusted chains on the swings.

"I can help with the funeral for yer mouse now, missy," Luke said. "I saw him so peaceful in yer old freezer with yer writin' on the inside of that box. I knew right away that he must be important to ye."

"Can you think of something poignant to say to an important dead mouse?" asked Shirley.

"Of course I can, missy," said Luke. "Are you ready?"

"I think so," said Shirley.

Luke remembered the Scottish prayer his mother recited when his father died.

Shirley sat in the grass next to Mouse—in the shade, under the sun, amid the cicadas, in the world—and bowed her head while Luke spoke.

"Deep peace of the running wave to ye
Deep peace of the flowing air to ye
Deep peace of the quiet earth to ye
Deep peace of the shining stars to ye
Deep peace of the infinite peace to ye:
To Shirley's dear little important Mouse."

"And to Harry," said a voice sniffling into a handkerchief.

It was Phillie. Phillie, who once again showed up when you least expected him.

"Do ye have anything to add to that, missy?" Luke asked. "And do you, Phillie?"

"I have something to add," said Phillie. "I heard that it's easier to get up to heaven if you have no shoes on. Harry didn't have any feet, so he's probably already there."

"All I have to add is thank you," said Shirley when Phillie had finished, "to Luke, to Phillie, and to Mouse." There wasn't much more to say that Shirley wanted anyone to hear.

To herself Shirley said: *I will not bury Mouse in the dirt. I will not burn him with the House of Wing matches. I will not toss him into Flushing Bay. I will let him gently roll out of the box and I will cover him with last year's leaves from the apricot tree that Grandma planted. Right here. And when Mouse disappears, he will become one with nature like Grandma says she will do one day. Mouse belongs here. And he will always belong to me. Like my father. Who always did and always will belong to me, too.*

EPILOGUE

LATE ONE SATURDAY AFTERNOON WHEN ANNA WAS AT A CLASS
for once-aspiring ballerinas at Madame Makarova's
Royal Academy of Ballet, Shirley sat at the dinette table
with her very own copy of *Pippi Longstocking*, studying
Astrid Lindgren's blowy cursive in a letter she had just
picked up at the library. The envelope was addressed to
Miss Chin, Children's Librarian, Main Street Library,
Queens, USA. Shirley opened it and read:

Dear Shirley Alice Burns,

Do not despair! I am sure that by now
you have discovered that your father, like
Pippi's, is everywhere: in the toes in your
shoes, in the dandelions in the field, in the

crows in the trees, in the sweetness of the cream puff inside your mouth, in the moon at night when you are in your bed. Even in the words you wrote to me. I can tell you are a writer from your letter. Then you must write. The world needs more people like you. Don't ever forget that.

With every good wish,
Astrid Lindgren
6 July 1961

P.S. I happen to think that "Shirley Alice Burns" is a fine name for a writer.

The book was a gift from Miss Chin. So was the letter, written on Shirley's birthday.

Shirley didn't hear the telephone when it rang, she was that enthralled by the words and the handwriting in front of her—so free and so feathery and so *not* perfect. The words had skipped off the pen, off the desk—off the dinette table, perhaps—of Astrid Lindgren. All the way to Queens from Sweden.

When Shirley finally realized the phone was ringing, she answered it. It was Anna, calling from a pay phone, saying she would be home late, that she had stopped to do some shopping on Austin Street for a new lipstick or a new nail polish. Anna had been much better with her money and was now contributing five dollars every two weeks to their ever-growing Attached House Fund, which Shirley had told her about. After Shirley had revealed her own stash of cash, ever growing from her various jobs. Anna's ship had still not come in.

· · · · ·

Some impossible wishes *do* come true. Anna, in a moment of weakness, said yes when Shirley asked for a dog. Natalie and Porky, at Aunt Claire's house in close quarters for two months, had made four distinguished-looking puppies! Some were black, some brown. Some were a little of each. You never can tell with genes.

And some impossible things *can* be fixed. Shirley skillfully scissored the one picture she had of herself and her father to fit the heart-shaped picture frame that Grandma had found in the trash. There was some space left over, so she put a picture of Anna in there, too. It was perfect.

· · · · ·

And Shirley wrote.

Sometimes at Anna's desk, sometimes in her bed,

sometimes outside on the stoop or at the Main Street Library. Some writers can write anywhere, using the voice that best suits what they are writing.

Once and Future Queens
By Shirley Alice Burns

Chapter 1

The very un-proper Princess Prunella rests upon her majestic throne with her royal dog, Sweet William, on an extraordinary morning in the Palace of Peace, where she practices her français (French for "French"—say: "frahn-say") while one Queen takes driving lessons on the royal driveway below and the other Queen sits regally sewing pin-striped baseball pants with pockets for the Princess. Sir Luke attends to the perfect emerald-green lawn outside, waiting patiently for Prunella to change out of her royal robe and help him fix the washing machine in the Attached Palace's laundry room.

Shirley smiled. She put down her pencil and got ready to meet Edie, who would be waiting for her exactly halfway from where each of them lived on Queens Boulevard. At six.